# THE Breathtaking Christa P

## A NOVEL OF CRIME

### BY

# P. Curran

CCB
New Orleans, LA

Crescent City Books is an imprint of Commonwealth Books, Inc. Distributed to the trade by NBN (National Book Network) throughout North America, Canada, and the U.K. Crescent City Books and its logo are registered trademarks of Commonwealth Books, Inc.


Joseph S. Phillips and Susan J. Wood, Ph.D., Publishers
www.blackwidowpress.com

THIS IS A WORK OF FICTION. Bars, stores, and restaurants are mentioned only for verisimilitude, not to disparage any actual business or its owners. No character in this book represents or depicts any real person, living or dead.

Cover and interior photography: Louis Maistros
Model: Mary Alice
Cover design & text production: Geoff Munsterman

ISBN-13: 978-1-7338924-9-0

Printed in the United States of America

# THE
# BREATHTAKING
# CHRISTA P

# 1

THE MORNING AFTER I ARRIVED IN NEW ORLEANS and delivered the Chrysler I'd driven down, I stepped out of a diner on Saint Charles Avenue and heard a man call my name, loud, and then repeat it. By the time I decided I shouldn't react I already had.

"It *is* you," Ennis said, as though I might not have known.

I shook his hand and asked him, I think, how he'd been. My mouth just ran on its own. Mentally I needed to gauge whether Ennis had any idea why I'd come south.

He didn't, I guessed. Any anxiety he showed more likely came from remembering how he'd last seen me, or from whatever he had on his mind before he spotted me. Or maybe his eyes always had that glint. I hadn't seen him in twenty years, and we'd only eaten lunch together for less than one semester of high school.

"So you live down here," Ennis said.

"Sure do. For now."

"When'd you move here?" He sounded very grown-up.

"I don't know, a while ago," I said with a shrug. I asked him what he did for a living, and while he told me I studied him: He dressed neatly and wore his hair short these days. Now *I* was the longhair with the knapsack, though not out of choice.

Ennis eyed my shirt, and I realized I had a work uniform on. So that would explain his nervousness, then. The school where I met him was a Catholic preparatory, from which most graduates went on to college.

I own three blue collared shirts, each with a different first name sewn onto its left breast. (I used to have a fourth one.) Strangers trust you when you wear a workshirt. Police tend not to notice you. Guys like

Ennis work hard to speak respectfully to you, because they don't want you to know they think you're somehow below them.

"Whereabouts you live down here?" Ennis asked me.

"Actually," I said, "I'm looking for a new place."

"Oh, yeah?" he said. "You know what you do? Go up to Gentilly Boulevard, by the racetrack."

I nodded, and my gaze drifted past his shoulder. A blonde girl came out of the drug store across Saint Charles. As she crossed the streetcar tracks towards us, she folded a prescription bag to fit inside her purse. Then her eyes met mine.

I don't know whether I flinched or what, but Ennis paused and turned, and greeted the girl, "Hey, Tara, come here. Want you to meet an old friend of mine."

She smiled at me. Ennis told her my first name. She seemed young for him, although Ennis and I were only thirty-four. He told me she'd just started law school at Tulane.

"Listen, what I was saying," Ennis went on, and the instant he turned back to face me Tara ditched her pleasant grin, "you should go up by the racetrack and look around there for a place. You'll find something, cheap. All these old white guys that got out of the service bought houses around there so they could go play the horses every day, and they don't want to rent to anyone black. I spent this past winter apartment-hunting for her—" He pointed his thumb at Tara. She flashed that grin at me again. "—and those are the best deals we've seen. It's just, you're not near anything. Cab to the Quarter costs five, six bucks."

Ennis told me how great it was to see me, then he took Tara's hand and led her inside the diner. I left.

Later, on the streetcar, I realized it had been twenty years to the exact day since I'd last seen Ennis, maybe even to the hour. I knew the date because the last time I'd seen him, the morning I got expelled in 1975, changed everything for me.

By contrast, Ennis probably didn't note the anniversary, but I knew that at their table in the diner he would describe that same long-ago day's events for Tara, unless he already had recounted them at some earlier point and could just say, *Remember that guy I told you about, he freaked out and beat a kid to death with a chair my freshman year in high school? That was him outside. It surprises me he's even allowed out on his own.*

Which I'm not.

# 2

ENNIS WAS RIGHT ABOUT THAT NEIGHBORHOOD by the racetrack, though. That afternoon I rode the Esplanade bus to Broad and walked to Gentilly. For a few blocks I didn't see anyone white. That didn't bother me; the best friend I ever had was black.

The corner stores advertised racing forms. All the homes had bars over their windows and iron gates on their doors, like everywhere else in New Orleans. I passed a park on the right, and then the racetrack was on my left, or at least its parking lot was. Beyond the parking lot a half-built grandstand towered several stories over any building in sight.

The horses weren't running that day. Later I learned that the season stopped at the end of March.

Across Gentilly from the racetrack's entrance stood a bar. As I came closer I saw that this bar had two separate rooms, and two separate entrances. I went in the farther one.

"Yeah?" a man I couldn't see asked me.

Scattered around the room, half a dozen people waited motionless for my answer.

"Can I help you?" the man said, louder. He stepped into view through the doorway to a storage area.

"I'll just have a coke, please," I said.

"We're closed," he said.

I glanced around. Half a dozen people still stared back.

"We're just cleaning up," the man explained. "For Jazz Fest. We open on Friday."

"Oh," I said. Everyone in the bar became busy: A woman standing on a chair went back to scraping tape marks off the front window, a man resumed sweeping the wood floor. In the adjacent bar something glass broke, and someone cursed.

"May I ask you a question?" I said, and the man nodded. "Do you know anywhere around here I could find a place to stay?"

"Around *here*?"

I said, "Yeah."

He looked wary. "I wouldn't know," he said, slowly. "Maybe there's, uh..."

"No one's going to rent to you," said the woman scraping the window. She hopped from her chair to the floor and wiped her hands on a rag as she spoke to me. "Every Jazz Fest, seventy million people from Los Angeles and New York decide they want to live on this block. Then they sleep it off."

"What does this jazz show have to do with it?" I asked, politely.

Again they all looked at me, more curious this time.

"You don't know what Jazz Fest is?" the guy behind the bar said.

"I just came to town," I said. "A friend of mine said he saw some good rental deals around here."

"Who's your friend?" the woman asked.

I swallowed, trying hard to remember his first name. No use. "Mister Ennis," I said.

"Oh, right, he was looking for a place for his girlfriend," she said. "I showed him two apartments."

I smiled and nodded. "I went to high school with him."

"And you call him 'Mister.'" She lit a cigarette.

"Actually, I forgot his name." No one wanted to hear. "High school was a long time ago."

She took a drag and said, "So, anyway, you need an apartment."

"Just a room," I said. "I don't have a job yet."

"You do now," she said, and led me out of the bar.

She took me inside her house, next door to the bar. Her name was Christine. She had to phone another woman, Alva, who didn't live in

New Orleans but who owned the bar and Christine's house and a bunch of others.

"Watch this," Christine said, dialing the phone. "Alva's going to complain that you're another Jazz Fest idiot."

Alva did just that. After a few minutes Christine mentioned Ennis's name. That won Alva over instantly.

"Of course," Christine said, her voice soothing. "Jazz Fest doesn't even start till the end of the week, Alva. Would I waste a dime calling you?" Soon they hung up.

Christine's house was what they call a shotgun shack; it had no hall, and the doors to each room lined up so that a slug fired straight through the front door would exit the back door without hitting a wall.

Christine took me out her back door into a large yard she shared with several other houses. As we stepped through the unmown grass it dawned on me that I didn't need this Alva checking my references. I wanted Ennis to forget ever seeing me in New Orleans.

I said, "So your landlady knows Ennis."

"I guess," Christine said.

"Where does she live?"

"Texas." Christine pointed at a six-foot plank fence that ran the perimeter of the yard, connecting all the houses. "Think you can fix that?"

"What's wrong with it?" I asked.

"Well, it's beat to shit," she said, surprised I had to ask. "Replace whatever planks are broken and paint the whole thing. Can you do that?"

"Sure," I said.

"That'll be your first week's rent, if you want," she said, and then, surveying the yard and tallying how much fence there was, added, "Or two weeks. That should be two weeks' worth. You ever work as a bouncer?"

I shook my head.

"Because you could work the door at the bar," she said. "Just the next two weekends. It'll be worth it. Cash."

"I can't."

"Whatever," she said.

"I hate violence," I said.

"You wouldn't have to do any," she told me, shrugging as she sized me from toe to crown. "You look big enough, nobody would start anything."

"But if they did," I said. I'm only six-one. Christine herself stood just under five foot. Often I appear tall to people, maybe because I get gaunt when I don't eat regularly.

Christine brought me into the rear two rooms of another shotgun, this one longer than hers. Someone old had lived here until recently, I could tell. A tacky coat of nicotine covered the walls and floor, and stained the white counter of the kitchenette a sickly yellow. For furniture I had two plaid armchairs and an end table, all of it scarred by cigarette burns. In the other room were a bureau and a bed. I dropped my knapsack on top of the bureau. Mounted on the wall beside the bed were two vertical steel tracks, four feet apart, with slots where you insert shelf brackets. Someone had sealed off a doorway with sheet rock to convert the house into two apartments.

"You scrub all this down, and paint it," Christine said. "And do you know anything about lawn mowers?"

"I used to do gardening," I told her, which was true.

"I have two lawn mowers, neither of them works," Christine said. "If you can get one of them running, and do the whole backyard out there, that'll pay your rent for the rest of your first month. After that, a hundred twenty-five. Plus part of the utility."

"That sounds fine," I said. "I don't need to fill out a lease, do I?"

Christine shook her head. "I been here two years, I still haven't."

Outside, as she led me back across the yard, I tried to think of a way to bring Ennis up again. Christine took me behind a garage, the only one on the property. It blended in because it matched the houses, which were all painted the same mustard color as the fence but with brown trim around their windows.

On the garage's back wall was a shed, a lean-to as high as my shoulder. Rain had warped the door, so we had to pry it open. No one had swept inside this shed in years. I could tell which gardening tools had joined the collection recently because placing them there had upset the dust and spiderwebs.

"What do you think?" she asked, lighting another smoke.

"I'd rather live in that house you just showed me," I said.

She dropped her cigarette.

I said, "I meant that as a joke. I'm sure this stuff will do fine. Is there a hardware store around here?"

"Yeah, right on Broad," she said, smiling. "You know how to keep a straight face."

While she picked her cigarette off the grass I knelt to examine the lawn mowers. They had gas engines.

"You can do the lawn every month as part of the rent," Christine said. "I have to talk to Alva, though. Let's wait until you've done it once, then I'll ask."

I stood and scratched my scalp. "You don't remember Ennis's first name, either?" I asked.

She shook her head.

As I closed the shed I said, "That's so embarrassing. I ran into him, and he knows me and I can't remember his first name. Sure hope I don't see him again."

"Uh-huh," Christine said, and started toward her back door.

I caught up with her and asked, "What apartments did you show him? The one I'm taking?"

"No," she said, "he wanted a whole house. It was for his girlfriend, and he doesn't want anyone near her. That's why he searched these neighborhoods far away from the Quarter or anyplace else—so no one will know her."

My face must have told her I was confused.

"She was a stripper," Christine explained. "She used to dance at Maiden Voyage when she first moved down here. Now he's putting her into law school, and he wants her someplace she can't get into trouble. He would rather have her live over here but it's too far from Tulane." She tipped her ash onto the grass. "Good luck, buddy. He better have deep pockets."

"I didn't know all that," I said. "I just met her. Hadn't seen Ennis in twenty years."

"Yeah, supposedly he's married, too," Christine added, holding the door open for me to follow her into her kitchen. "I was glad she didn't want to live here—the girlfriend, I mean. She had a dog, and I hate them."

"So how does Ennis know your landlady?"

"He doesn't, really," she said. "He just made a good impression on her. Alva doesn't know this stuff about his mistress. I just heard that from some dancers. They're like washwomen."

I let the topic go. What she'd said sounded as reassuring as I could expect, short of asking, *Alva won't check with him about me, will she?* Besides, even if the landlady did call Ennis, he might not tell her what happened at school. It hadn't kept him from saying hello to me.

Inside her living room, Christine took a ceramic waterpipe from a cabinet and offered it to me.

"No, thank you," I said.

"You don't smoke?"

"No," I said. "Drugs affect me badly."

"Mind if I do?" she asked.

I told her to go right ahead. She took a long pull off the pipe and exhaled away from me. The smoke wafted out an open window, between the bars, to the sidewalk.

"Want me to shut that window?" I asked her.

She shook her head while drawing another lungful. When she finished, before she released it, she said, "I know a cop."

Christine's mood turned glum after that.

I went back into the bar. The guy I'd first talked to, Cody, offered me six bucks an hour to paint one wall stained by the leaky roof. When I finished that, I waxed the bar. After four hours he gave me thirty bucks. He bought hamburgers for everyone, too. First food I'd eaten since the diner where I'd met Ennis that morning.

# 3

The Jazz Fest started that Friday.

Cody insisted that I work the door, even when I swore I couldn't fight. "You won't have to," he promised me. "We ain't had a problem yet. People just sometimes feel too good, and then *I* handle them."

I'd spent the previous two days cleaning my two rooms. I scrubbed the floor and walls. I soaked the venetian blinds in the tub. Christine showed me that I had three sets of linen in a closet, and said we would get the paint for the fence on Monday, after the first weekend of the Jazz Fest.

This concert was like Christmas for this neighborhood.

So I worked the door at the bar. At eleven each morning swarms of white people marched or drove onto the Fairgrounds, and from late afternoon until the concert ended around seven, I sat on a stool taking five dollars from each customer in exchange for a stamp on the right hand. Concertgoers packed the bar, and a rock band started at about six-thirty. Everyone treated me very nicely. I think most of them had eaten LSD.

Sunday night a squadcar pulled up outside Christine's. I told Cody, and he told me to ignore it. "That's," he started, and then paused to rephrase what he hadn't said. "That's someone Christine knows."

Monday Christine slept all day, or at least stayed inside, so we didn't go buy paint. That afternoon I got both of her mowers running. The older one actually worked better; someone must have replaced the rotor blades. I mowed the entire lawn, then I went inside and scrubbed the inside of my refrigerator, which was a cheap model yet fairly new.

Inside the shed I found a scythe, its blade unrusted but too dull to use, and pruning shears. Christine hadn't mentioned trimming the trees that hung over the fence, so I figured I could surprise her.

In the alley beside my house I introduced myself to Pat, the old sailor who lived in the front. "Good to meet you," Pat told me, shaking my hand. He and the neighborhood's other remaining white guys drank at some bar a few blocks away, and he invited me to join him. "I mean, it ain't just an old man's joint. There's broads there and whatnot."

Rather than confess that I didn't drink, I thanked him and said I'd make it by sooner or later. I walked with Pat down Gentilly until we reached the shop where he bought his racing form and his cigars. He steered me toward a seafood store on Broad. I bought three pounds of boiled shrimp and two pounds of crawfish, a type of miniature lobster they boil in spicy broth. The clerk showed me how to eat them. I also got a six-pack of root beer. I carried it all home and ate in my clean kitchenette.

Tuesday at noon Christine answered her door cheerfully. I already knew her well enough not to ask about the previous day. She drove me to buy paint, and let me pick my own colors for my rooms.

"Might as well buy the same color as the fence," I suggested. "This way I can use any that's left over."

"For Christ's sake," she said. "Pick cameo white or something. You can't mix indoor and outdoor paint, anyway. The fence'll warp."

So I spent the rest of Tuesday painting my apartment cameo white. It gave both rooms a new soft quality. Christine brought me over a small plug-in radio, so I listened to jazz music while I painted. Now and then I thought about Christine a little.

When I moved the refrigerator to paint behind it, I found the brackets and wooden shelves that belonged to the steel tracks on the bedroom wall. I brought them inside. The shelves didn't fit; they were nine feet long, and the two steel tracks where I had to hang the brackets were only four feet apart. A vertical line of three screw holes in the plaster marked the spot where someone had ripped a third track from the wall. Later I painted over the screw holes.

Wednesday I painted a few sections of the fence that did not need repairs, and sized up the parts that did. A few planks I would replace altogether, and one square post as well, but I didn't pry those down yet. No sense luring burglars into the yard.

In the evening I walked around the block to knock on Christine's front door. The squadcar had pulled up on her lawn, so instead I went hiking along Gentilly, and ate a hamburger outside a drive-through on Saint Bernard, a mile or so from my house. Not a lot of white people ate at this place, I could tell.

When I came home, the squadcar still sat there outside Christine's. A couple of times that night I thought I heard shouting inside her house. I might have imagined it.

On Thursday Jazz Fest started again. I worked the door at the bar again that night. More of the concertgoers seemed to come from New Orleans this time. I didn't see Christine all day, and when I asked Cody about her, he said, "Look, I'll talk to you another time about Christine, all right? Not now."

While the band played, a man named Gary who was high on something came outside for air and began telling me Jazz Fest stories. The funniest one involved his friend Terry whose pill-addled mother-in-law owned a world-class restaurant in the French Quarter. One night after Jazz Fest Terry showed up at the restaurant wearing sandals, soiled BVD briefs, and a Dr. Seuss hat, so stoned on acid he couldn't remember why he'd come.

Finally Gary caught a cab home. Everyone left by ten. Cody handed me a bag of crawfish and paid me through midnight.

I ate in my kitchenette. Midway through the bag, I wrapped it up and stuck it in my fridge. I washed my hands twice, and still my fingers stank of whatever spice they boil the crawfish in.

I stepped out the back and crossed the yard to Christine's. She had all her lights out, but as I came closer I saw a candle burning in her bedroom. I knew which room she slept in, because she'd brought me through the house, so I knocked on her window.

"What do you want?" she asked calmly.

I told her it was me.

"I know who it is," she said. "What do you want?"

"I just wanted to see you," I told her. "I was wondering if you were all right. You haven't been around."

"I'm fine," she said.

I stood there in the dark.

"You want to come in?" she asked.

Shifting from foot to foot, I said, "Only if it's okay. I didn't mean to wake you."

"I'm not sleeping. Go around back."

With her candle in an old-fashioned brass holder she let me in the kitchen door and led me to her room.

"Have a seat," she said, and dropped onto her bed. "Ever do coke?"

"No," I told her, and squatted upon the floor.

"Then maybe you shouldn't watch this," Christine said. From her nightstand she picked up a syringe.

To shoot coke, you have to mainline it. If you put that stuff under your skin anywhere but in a vein, you get an abscess. It's a giant pimple that won't heal, that in fact keeps swelling until you lose your arm. That's rare in the regular world, but I've seen a number of them, usually from a sloppy shot that happened by accident during a binge. The discharge from a coke abscess smells bad enough to put you off food.

Junkies never go to the doctor until a limb rots off or someone dies, and a coke fiend will keep at it even longer than that. They disrupt any ward that admits them. One guy I knew for a few weeks survived a bacterial infection that ate through his heart. He and his friends all mixed their coke with tap water to shoot it, and microbes in the water attacked them. All his friends died from cardiac ulcers.

Doing coke must feel terrific. Even someone who narrowly escapes death will go back to it. I've only ever taken drugs if a nurse stayed to make sure I took them, and that only happened a few times. I don't even like to take aspirin.

After Christine finished injecting herself, she dabbed blood off her arm with a tissue. Her pupils dilated into black marbles. Thankfully I couldn't see her face well by candlelight. Dolls scare me.

"I painted some of the fence today," I told her.

Christine nodded, just barely, and made a warm grunt in her throat.

"We need some planks, though," I said. "Do you know a lumberyard we can go to?"

She kept nodding.

"I'm going to need a hammer, too," I said.

"I've got a hammer," she said. Speaking at all taxed her.

"Oh, okay."

We sat in the dark some more. Moonlight began to enter her room, though she didn't notice.

"I thought you were going to try and fuck me," she said.

I didn't say: *That kind of talk bothers me.* I said, "No. I don't expect I can just come over and knock on your window for, for stuff like that."

"I used to be a whore," Christine said.

I shut up.

"I used to fuck guys I'd never seen before, just so I could shoot coke," she said. "I liked it better than what I do to get coke now."

Christine told me about the cop. Wayne was his name. Supposedly she'd gotten a restraining order against Wayne, and it had proven useless because he was a cop. Her version of events sounded very slightly improbable to me. Women in that position sometimes make things up or embellish them, I don't know why. She claimed Louisiana didn't have a law against stalkers, and that the fact she had slept with him voluntarily a few times before he started beating her mitigated whatever legal help she could request. I couldn't imagine that.

No point saying so, though. I just listened. When I did start to speak I caught myself likening her situation to a patient getting abused by orderlies, so I shut up. Luckily the coke kept Christine from analyzing what I'd begun saying.

When she fell quiet I got to my feet and studied the wall above her dresser, where she'd hung a dozen small handbills and newspaper ads for nightclubs. Every one mentioned "The Breathtaking Christa P." A few included a photograph that in the weak light took me a few seconds to recognize as Christine wearing a platinum blonde wig.

"I used to sing," she explained, staring into her candle's flame.

"I'd like to hear you sometime," I said.

"I don't anymore," she told me. "I used to sing in hotel lounges and places like that."

Throughout the night her mood peaked and ebbed, and toward daylight she abruptly asked me to go home. I rose to my feet and went. At her back door she hugged me. Then she went inside and shot the rest of her coke.

# 4

THE REST OF THE JAZZ FEST PASSED. Friday afternoon I read a schedule that someone had left in the bar, and it surprised me to see how many different musicians performed each day. Even though the concert went on from morning until evening, they must have each only played one or two songs.

Cody asked if I wanted to see the show with him on Saturday. I declined. I tried to bring Christine up with him, but he begged off. "She's my friend," he said, as if that excused him.

Sunday at midnight after we closed the bar I went for a walk. Everyone I'd worked with these past two weekends sat inside the bar now with the curtains drawn and the doors locked. Sitting there with them as they grew drunker and drunker could upset me, so I decided to hike all the way around the perimeter of the racetrack.

After a while I reached a spot where someone's yard stopped me from following the racetrack's white fence directly. The way they laid the grounds out made the track seem pentagonal in shape, but I believe the angle of adjacent streets caused this illusion, that it was really a lopsided diamond.

My course brought me past a bayou—which is a river that doesn't move; I only knew what to call it because Christine had mentioned that one lay nearby—and then onto Esplanade Avenue. I walked until I reached a group of stores, when the racetrack reappeared on my left. Lots of papers and cups and cans littered the streets.

By this time all the stores had closed except a Circle K one block further down Esplanade, so I went there to buy a soda. They had gas pumps out front. A befuddled white fellow wearing a hat with feathers jutting from its band watched me cross the parking lot and enter the store. He stood between a bank of payphones and a dumpster.

That guy gave me the creeps. After I paid for my root beer, rather than pass him again, I walked around the block the other way.

But instead of the racetrack I found a closed laundromat. A roach two inches long patrolled the inward surface of its front window. Inside, another bug of similar size scurried across several light-colored washing machines.

Alongside the laundromat, another street ran behind the Circle K, and where it ended three blocks away I again saw the white fence of the racetrack. The mysterious way these roads connected, how they ran neither parallel nor perpendicular, threw me. Where I grew up, streets followed a rigid grid except where natural obstacles defied them.

As I set off toward the white fence a dog darted into the street to flee my path. I thought it might belong to someone who lived nearby. Then it wandered under a streetlight, and I saw its bloated, dangling teats, the mange eating its fur. It wore no collar.

At the first corner stood the bar that Pat had invited me to. It had closed already. The owner had no gates over the picture windows. Inside, stools rested upside-down atop tables. Unlike the bar next to Christine's, this one opened every day, all year round.

Midway down the cross street another stray picked at something on the ground. At the next corner the cross street had better lighting, and I saw a group of four or five dogs fighting over a tattered paper bag.

Garbage, I realized. On this side of the track was another gate where pedestrians entered and exited the Jazz Fest. Thousands leaving the concert had dumped half-eaten food onto the pavement, and in their wake roamed these dogs.

When I reached the white fence I saw a car zip past inside the racetrack parking lot. In the gutter to my left, a patchy chow assessed me as harmless, then resumed licking the mouth of a discarded can of beer. From here a long low building fifty yards inside the fence blocked my view of the track itself, and it occurred to me that the track hadn't been visible from anywhere else around the perimeter, either.

I tried to picture the track set up with a stage in its grass oval center and all the food concessions Cody had told me about. Maybe I should have gone with him on Saturday to see it, but crowds often upset me.

Strangely, somebody had swept the trash on this street into piles, and then left the piles heaped against the fence. On reflex I scanned the first trash I saw, checking what I could eat, but then I touched the money in my pocket through my jeans and stopped myself. Aside from what I had earned from Cody, I still had most of what the guy at the chop shop had paid me for the Chrysler.

The grandstand loomed over the entire neighborhood. From this side I could see the ladders and materials on the roof where the workmen had stored them for the weekend. The grandstand resembled a mammoth aluminum barn.

A footfall startled me.

I spun and found a black dog behind me. He tottered in place, head bowed, ears back flat, tail swinging furiously from side to side. One of his parents had been a pit bull, the other something lop-eared with a pretty coat. He stood only knee-high at the shoulder, partly from starving but also because he was less than a year old.

His dirty part-sheepdog companion waited a dozen feet away, doubtful that I wouldn't thrash them both.

Instantly I knew their names: This one who'd approached me was Stupid, and the shaggy one was Useless. That's what the orderlies used to call me and Yusef.

I offered my palm; and Stupid licked it.

"Hey," I said. "How you doing?"

Stupid sat, and cocked his head. His ears relaxed. Conjunctivitis oozed from his right eye. Had he the power of speech, he would have said, *I don't understand. I'm hungry all the time, and people kick me if I eat their garbage. Tell me what I'm supposed to do, and I'll do whatever it is. I don't deserve slow death on the street.*

We stayed that way for a long time, still but for Stupid's tail, which thumped the ground every so often.

"Come on," I said finally, and walked toward home.

Both dogs immediately fell into stride alongside me. By the time we'd covered half the distance to Gentilly Boulevard, they'd both adopted that panting smile dogs get. I walked quickly, figuring if I caught Cody before he went home, he could drive me to a supermarket to buy food for them.

A block from Gentilly I stopped. The dogs stared at me.

Christine hated dogs. She'd told me so. She didn't want them in the yard. That's why she didn't want Ennis's mistress for a neighbor.

"No," I said. Stupid and Useless stared at me. "No," I repeated, and stamped my foot.

I took off, and they made to follow, uncertain. I stamped again. "No!" I snarled. Useless seemed readier to accept this turn, as though he'd never believed me to start with. Stupid took it more personally. He threw his ears back and shook all over, snuffling and whining.

I went to Christine's. She and I watched television. Neither of us mentioned Thursday night. After an hour or so I asked if she wanted to go to the lumberyard in the morning. She shook her head, so I asked her where I could get tools sharpened.

The next day I woke at noon. I took the scythe from the shed and carried it to the hardware store on Broad. Near the park, I glimpsed Useless or a dog very much like him eating from a toppled trash can. I looked away quickly, before his partner could scamper into view.

To me, a hardware store should always have soft light and a floor of dark wood worn smooth by generations of customers. Its air should reek of machine oil. For all I know, the last hardware store like that closed before 1980.

This one on Broad had a bright tile floor and shiny metal shelves. The anonymous air in the place could have come from a post office or an emergency room, and both the woman behind the register and the clerk manning the aisles could work at either.

"I need this sharpened," I said to the clerk, who gave a mute nod and carried my scythe into a back room. A thick door swung shut behind him, yet it only partially muffled the screech of a grinding stone.

"You new down here?" the woman asked me.

I nodded.

"Where you move from?"

"Australia," I said.

"Oh, really?" She seemed impressed.

"Sure thing," I said. "I moved there in 1983, and just came back."

"Must have been an interesting place to live," she said. "Did you live in a city or up in the mountains?"

"A city," I said. "New Liverpool. Very nice place."

She smiled. The guy brought my scythe back, and I paid the woman. As I stepped out the door, I spotted a sign on the front window: HELP WANTED. I went back inside and asked the woman about it. She summoned a man named Pierre from the back room.

"You ever work in hardware before?" Pierre asked me.

"I sure have," I told him, which was almost true. "My grandfather had a hardware store where I grew up."

"Oh, yeah? Where's that?" He liked me already.

I picked, "Wisconsin." No one would check.

I told Pierre I could work any hours he wanted. Some college kid had gone home for the summer, and they needed another afternoon clerk.

The man who'd honed my scythe cut in, "Yeah, I'm just the morning guy. I been working doubles for a week."

"And he bitches," Pierre said, "so I want someone in here who's got some hair on his ass. Fill out an application." He handed me two sheets of photocopied paper. One stated company policy, the other asked for information.

My mistake. I should have gone home first, then come back to ask about the job. That way I would have had my identity straight. The name and social security number I knew I could use were on a card I kept safe in my knapsack. Since Christine hadn't made me sign a lease, I hadn't looked at the card in over a week, so I'd forgotten the name.

"Listen," I said, "I just happened to be coming through here; I'm in the middle of a bunch of errands. Can I fill this out at home and bring it tomorrow?"

"Sure, go ahead," Pierre said. He pointed at his clerk and said, "This here's Freddy, and that's my wife, Edith. I'm Pierre Richard." We shook hands.

All three of them stared, waiting to learn my name.

*I'm Stupid.* "I'm Whitey,'" I said, since it was the name on my shirt.

Pierre said, "Hey, ain't we all?" and burst out laughing. "All right, Whitey, bring that with you tomorrow, and you can start around one."

"What's your real name?" Edith asked.

I pretended not to hear her. A customer opened the door and stepped in. I took the door from him and said, "I'll see you all tomorrow."

Which I wouldn't, as it turned out.

# 5

THAT NIGHT A STORM BROKE. It had rained often without notice since I'd come to New Orleans, but this time the sky opened. Water pounded my roof in torrents.

It woke me. I got out of bed and switched on my radio. Nothing came out. I tried the lights. Dead.

I didn't have candles, unless the previous tenant had left some hidden in a drawer. Waiting here alone without light in a dead man's home could have upset me if I hadn't already repainted the place.

Sheets of water pelted my windows. It grew denser by the minute. I feared the panes might shatter. If any moon hung in the heavens, I couldn't locate the faintest trace of it.

I sat in an armchair and marveled that the sky had been clear as ice when I'd come in from working in the yard earlier. I'd made a point of checking, because I needed to know whether I could leave the tools out so I could work more after dinner. Christine had fried some chicken. Afterward, since she had plans to meet someone in the French Quarter and couldn't spare the time to wrap the stuff herself, she had given me all the leftovers to put in my refrigerator...and then I'd lain in bed and forgotten about the tools outside, until this very second.

I pulled on an undershirt and my pants and boots and bolted out my door. The instant I stepped into the rain it drenched me.

At the bottom of my steps my feet plunged into what I mistook at first for a puddle but was in fact a tide. A lake had filled the yard.

With my pupils adjusted fully, I could see maybe six foot ahead, and every few seconds I needed to wipe the rain from my eyes. The shallowest area I crossed reached high above my ankles. Clumsily I followed the fence to the spot where I'd left the tools propped against it. I hadn't even used the scythe yet.

The storm had knocked the scythe flat on the ground, so I groped around beneath the water and found it. Then I grabbed the shears and set off across the blackness, pushing my way through sheets of rain, blindly trying to judge where the shed lay. I knew Christine kept a flashlight in there, though I hadn't tested it to see whether it worked.

Instead of the shed I found the front corner of the garage. The water ran deeper on this side of the yard. I sloshed alongside the garage toward the sunken lean-to. Rather than set them down in the water again, I placed the scythe and the shears on the little roof.

The shed door scraped open more easily than usual. Inside the shed, the flashlight rested half-submerged upon the baseboard. By a miracle, it worked. To protect the batteries I held the flashlight under the shed's roof, out of the rain; a small amount of liquid had already leaked inside the lens chamber, painting a weird shifting arc along the bottom of the bright circle where the beam met the wall.

It made no sense to store the scythe and the shears in the shed. The water would keep rising. I played the flashlight outward across the yard, and could see no grass anywhere. The bucketloads dropping from above each second kept three or four inches of splash roiling upon the flood's surface.

I stuffed the flashlight into the waist of my jeans and pulled my shirt over it. Then one by one I pulled out every tool I could carry: a whipsaw, a hoe, an edger that probably didn't work, a pick hatchet. Last I found a pair of work gloves, which I hadn't noticed earlier but knew I ought to wear when using the saw or the scythe. I tucked the gloves in my waistband next to the flashlight and hauled the pile of tools over to my house. Along the way I stumbled and nearly tripped upon the uneven ground below the water.

At my house I bounded up the steps and set the tools inside. Just as I was about to race back to the shed for the lawnmowers, I changed my mind. It wasn't worth dragging each one through the murk and up my stairs. Gas mowers survive floods. Someone just has to dry them out.

So I stayed in my house. As soon as I shut the door behind me I became aware of how hard the rain had pelted my scalp and skin. At my kitchen counter I tried to squeeze my clothes a little dry. The amount of water in my hair alone surprised me. The work gloves were soaked.

For a short while I returned to the window, still dripping, to shine the flashlight out there. Only in the Bible had I heard of weather so intense as what I had just waded through. When I encounter something bizarre I have to double-check what I see, because I often go for days on end with little sleep or food. Usually that makes me calm and lucid, but it can also put me in a state where I need to question my impressions.

But no, this rain really fell in a deluge. No exaggeration, I could not see Christine's house. The flashlight's beam fought its way a scant dozen feet into the downpour and drowned there.

Somebody knocked on the rear wall of my apartment, the sealed doorway.

I walked into my bedroom and called out, "Hello?"

"Yeah, it's Pat," he called out. "I got candles, if you need some."

"I do," I said. "Hold up, I'll come around the side."

I tucked the flashlight back into my jeans and went out my side door into the alley. The eave shielded my head somewhat. Without the distraction of rain spattering my skull full-force, I noticed instead the roar the storm made. It teemed upon the top cement landing outside Pat's side door. I couldn't see the steps themselves.

Pat opened his door and said, "I heard you moving shit around in there, figured you's looking for the fusebox."

"No, it's a blackout," I said, climbing the steps to his door. "Even the racetrack's out."

As I crossed the threshold, I caught a rush of that tobacco aroma I'd scrubbed out of my own apartment. Pat had a cigar in his mouth. He led me inside.

He had three rooms instead of two, so in the middle one Pat had made himself a parlor. In one corner stood a leather recliner, aimed at the television. Three candles burned in this room—one on an end table beside the recliner, one on the mantle, and one on a coffee table in front of a small sofa—each stuck into the mouth of an empty Dixie Beer bottle.

"Yeah, they said that on the radio. Phone's out, too. News says it's a total fuckup out there. They got the highway backed up by the airport. Here," he said, waving a hand at the sofa, "you want to sit down awhile?"

"I'm soaked, Pat," I said. "I'll ruin your couch."

"Fuck it, sit on that chair, then," he said. The chair he meant was an armless wooden one with a straight back. "You want a beer?"

"No, thanks," I said.

"Well, if I'm awake at this hour, I need one," he said, and disappeared into the adjacent room.

By candlelight I had to squint to make out the pictures on his walls: mementos from the navy. I came closer. Most were black-and-white shots of ships, some with crewmen smiling and waving.

On the end table beside the recliner, the candle rested upon a stack of magazines. The top one was called *Chic*, and beneath its logo ran the tagline, "The best women...the best way."

Over the couch he'd hung photos of people. Pat himself appeared in about half of these. An eight-by-ten that dominated the gallery showed a dark-skinned girl emerging naked from the surf onto a white beach. This picture dated from much earlier than most old nudes I'd seen, certainly longer ago than any showing a woman's pubis so bluntly, but the image did not feel old because the girl's hair clung dripping to her shoulders rather than in some recognizable hairstyle. Up close I could see she was Japanese or something.

"Nice, huh?" Pat said from behind me. He dropped into his recliner, shoved out the leg rest. "Should've married that one, let me tell you. Why the fuck I ever left the Philippines I *don't* know."

Pat had brought his radio in. It ran on batteries. He placed it on the end table and switched it on. A newsman finished reading ball scores, and then a tire commercial came on. Pat puffed contentedly on his cigar.

The top story was the flood. It had wreaked mayhem in all the neighboring parishes. No one had anticipated the storm. A list of main routes where hordes of motorists had ditched their cars continued long enough that the newsman stumbled over words three different times.

"You know what's the ballbuster?" Pat asked me.

"What's that?"

"Esplanade is dry," he said, shaking his head. "Esplanade Ridge is the highest point in Orleans Parish. Every time we get flooded, Esplanade is fine, six blocks away."

"This happens a lot, then?" I asked.

Pat shrugged. "Once every, like, five years. This one's bad, though, from what they're saying. Nobody heard nothing about this, it just fell out of the sky. If it keeps up we're fucked. I had the water come in here before, a few times. Wrecked my couch and shit."

I nodded.

"It kills all those bums," he told me. "You know, they don't keep records on how many bums live here, there, or wherever. They don't know how many bums die in something like this. Especially down here, the rats and the bugs'll pick the body clean before the water's gone all the way down, even. See, bums try to sleep in places where these kids can't roll them."

The newsman began a story about private militias and how to tell the different ones apart. Most of the groups he described sounded identical to me.

"And the strays, too," Pat added, and took a pull off his beer.

I tried to follow the radio, but then I abruptly asked Pat, "What?"

After he swallowed, Pat said, "The strays—dogs and cats. They die in these floods. You watch, there's going to be dead animals on the ground after the water dries up. One time I had a whole bunch of cats drown right under the house. Stunk all that summer." He cleared his throat in disgust and drank some more beer.

Pat gave me a box of candles and wouldn't accept any money for them. I didn't argue with him. I didn't say so, but I was going out.

❀ ❀ ❀

Despite the blackout I could still find the traffic island on Gentilly Boulevard, so I walked on it through the squalling rain. In every direction cars lay paralyzed. A block and a half toward Esplanade, the street that bordered the racetrack emerged from the water. The slight incline Pat had mentioned made the blacktop visible at a distance, even with the streetlamps and houses out. I waded off the island in that direction.

When I reached the unflooded road, I found it actually more treacherous to walk. That same foamy layer of splash kicked up where the water landed, yet the slant made the street a conduit. All the rain that fell between here and Esplanade rushed downhill to collect at Gentilly. Up here this shallow cascade threatened my footing.

Lights shone inside some of the houses I passed, mostly candles. Inside one living room burned a full menorah, no doubt obtained at a junk sale or left in the house by a previous owner. A rat's corpse floated downstream past my feet.

I turned left, and around the next corner I could see headlights pass in the distance, and streetlamps. Esplanade had power.

Against the flow I trudged toward the lights. The pressure this storm exerted upon my body began to scramble me. Weather that extreme isolates me, and I have to avoid letting myself get claustrophobic.

Reaching the busy avenue did in fact lessen that pressure. Cars flew by, drivers desperately improvising new routes, seeking passable roads.

In the gutter lay a dark-colored carcass killed by a car, either hurled aside by impact or kicked there to keep the road clear. The dead creature wore no collar.

A small park faced me across Esplanade. Several dogs there cowered beneath a gnarled tree. I crossed and approached them. I counted five in all. The two pluckiest darted away into the rain, but the other three stayed prone on the wet ground, happy for whatever cover the tree provided. None of the dogs looked familiar. I set off for the bayou.

Soon the rain let up. A preternatural stillness took its place, especially since no cars were traveling along the bayou. More dogs roamed the streets, ripping at garbage bags. The flood had chased them here from other neighborhoods.

The bayou itself had risen. From a wooden footbridge I watched giant red-brown rats relocate their nest. My flashlight terrified them.

Finally I headed back toward Esplanade. This time the road I chose brought me to the Circle-K. The store itself was dark, but the tall lights in the parking lot worked. I noticed two employees and a guard inside, all waiting with their arms folded. A sheet of paper torn from a spiral notebook hung taped inside the glass door.

Stupid trotted out from behind the dumpster, near the bank of pay-phones.

I spotted him right away. He stopped at the curb and stared balefully at the cars speeding past. Useless followed, a dozen paces behind him.

Then Stupid began picking up and dropping his feet nervously, and I knew he meant to cross, to reach the park.

"No!" I shouted.

Both dogs looked at me.

"No!" I barreled across Esplanade, my hands outstretched. Brakes screamed beside me. A driver yelled something, I paid him no attention. In the lane closer to the dogs another driver stopped to let me cross.

At first the dogs didn't know who I was. Rain erases a lot of the scents they use to recall things.

# 6

IT TOOK ME A LONG TIME TO PERSUADE THE DOGS to follow me into the water so we could cross Gentilly. At last they came. The flashlight may have swayed them.

The storm had passed for good. Stars filled the firmament, their number swelled by the blackout; in their queer, faint light, the new calm heightened the strangeness of fording a sunken boulevard to reach home. Useless traveled at his normal slovenly gait, while Stupid imitated a horse in a river, his head bobbing as he moved, trusting with all his might that the water would not become deeper than he was tall.

At the traffic island Stupid's nerve gave completely. He whinnied. With the flashlight off and tucked back in my jeans, I picked the dog up and carried him. Useless followed us.

So as not to wake Pat, I opened the gate quietly and set Stupid on the landing outside Pat's side door. Already I felt a flea bite on my arm. Useless joined us at his own speed. I shut the gate and went down the passage to unlock my side door, assuming I'd need my hands free to carry Stupid inside, yet when I turned back I saw both dogs making their way toward me.

Together they climbed the steps into my apartment. I followed them inside and shut the door.

In my fridge I had four pieces of Christine's chicken. I cleaned the meat from three of them and divided it into two piles. It wasn't very much, so I smeared peanut butter onto some slices of cheese.

Watching the dogs eat, I thought they must suspect this meal was a dream. I examined them by candlelight. If nothing else, the cloudburst had given them a good bath.

They ate quickly and reclined on the floor beside the sink. Now that he'd escaped the river, Stupid wouldn't allow me to pick him up. That's a trait common to street animals. They snap at anyone who grabs them from a direction they can't watch.

Neither Stupid nor Useless could believe their luck. They only slept for short periods, and every so often I would notice one or the other's head perk up to study me as I sat in my armchair. The trip out to Esplanade and back had rankled me. I couldn't go back to bed anytime soon.

After a while I rose from my chair to stretch. As I yawned I looked out my back window.

A light moved across a wall somewhere inside Christine's house.

At first I doubted I had actually seen that. Then the light played across the window in the room beside her kitchen.

I couldn't imagine how she'd managed to make it home.

"Stay put, guys," I said to the dogs, and grabbed a dry shirt from my closet. I can't stand putting on wet jeans and I didn't want to soak my other pair crossing the flood, so I went out in my boxer shorts. They were too dark a color to look like underwear, anyway, least of all at night.

Before I left my house I blew the candle out. The dogs watched me go out my back door.

The yard had become a giant mirror laid flat. Every star in the sky shimmered back at itself from below. Now, with the storm departed, whatever noise I made entering the pool echoed off the fence around me. It made me self-conscious right away. As I crossed the yard I moved my legs straight ahead in the water, slowly, to avoid splashing. I skated along the grass underneath.

An owl appeared, unearthly gray and bigger than any I'd ever seen. It circled me twice and left. It occurred to me as I watched the bird vanish that the flood placed small mammals at the mercy of predators.

Nothing else happened while I crossed the yard. I began to feel silly for not moving more quickly.

When I got about ten feet from Christine's back door, my feet found her unfinished patio under the water. Had I walked faster, I could have broken a toe.

Just for a second, light flashed through the small diamond window in Christine's back door. She was in the kitchen now.

I lifted my foot carefully from the water and mounted the first step, then the second. The window measured maybe a foot at its widest, and I had to raise up onto my toes to see inside.

The person with the flashlight was too tall to be Christine. The hands I could see appeared to belong to a man, a white man rummaging through Christine's freezer.

He took out a rolled plastic package six inches long and buttoned it inside his left breast pocket. Then he shut the freezer door, which I hadn't realized was blocking my view. The flashlight accidentally showed him now, though not his face: a heavy guy in a police uniform.

On reflex I hopped directly to the ground.

The water splashed, loud. I clung to the side of the house.

The flashlight shone out through the diamond. The handle bumped the window frame as he trained the beam downward to check the steps.

For one long moment, all held still.

But he knew I was out there, I can't say how. First I heard a bolt sliding, then he tried the knob. The door held. It gave a frantic rattle. He'd meant to surprise me. I took off for the garage.

My first instinct led me toward my apartment, but Wayne got the door open behind me. He shouted for me to halt. Instead I darted around the garage so he lost sight of me, and then I made the next turn, to the side where the shed was. I thought I might crawl inside it.

Wayne didn't give me a chance. He splashed louder than a water buffalo. The havoc came toward me around the building. Rather than pry open the shed, I hoisted myself onto its roof and pressed my back against the garage.

At my feet lay the scythe and the pruning shears. Earlier, when I'd carried all the tools inside my house, I'd forgotten the two things I'd come out into the rain to save in the first place.

His flashlight silhouetted the corner of the garage beside me as Wayne drew near. Most of the noise subsided. He crept right up to the corner. In a second he would peer around it.

I hurled the pruning shears high in the air over the roof of the garage. They splashed down somewhere behind him, and Wayne spun around toward the sound.

He held quiet for an instant, after which he began to say something, probably a demand that I show myself. Whatever was on Wayne's mind, the scythe cut off his sentence when it cut off his head.

# 7

FOR A FEW MINUTES I WAS UPSET, BUT THEN I came to grips with my situation: I needed to get rid of Wayne's body, and I had to make sure no one knew where he'd died.

I dragged it by its feet across the yard. The water made dragging the thing easier. The toughest part was hauling it up the steps into my apartment. Wayne must have weighed two hundred fifty pounds. Stupid and Useless greeted me, very excited. They didn't know what to make of the parcel I'd brought home. Wayne wore chest-high black rubber waders like the ones my grandfather used to wear when we went fishing. The wet rubber reflected the light from my candles.

Then I had to go back outside and get Wayne's head. By the time I reentered my kitchen, the dogs were licking blood from the linoleum. The stump of his neck didn't bleed much, though. It had probably bled profusely after I first chopped his head off, while I was upset to the point of shock, and now his veins had lost their pressure.

So I took care of it. A plan had formed in my mind already.

The sun had all but risen by the time I came home from dumping it. Stupid and Useless sure were glad to see me. I had bought actual dog food, too.

When someone becomes your friend, sooner or later this person tells you something weird, and how you react decides the course of your friendship. Usually it's about sex or shitting or something close to those. The fact that I don't react well to personal exhibitions of that type has a lot to do with why I've had hardly any friends in my life.

I've always seen people differently than most others do. Probably there are a certain number in the general population who share this talent with me; I just haven't met many of them. I believe this way of seeing accounts for the horrible things people sometimes get caught doing. I know it's been responsible for the worst things I've ever done.

They used to let Yusef read *Boys' Life*. His cousin would buy these tawdry crime magazines and staple them inside *Boys' Life* covers for him. Only Yusef and I knew about this scam. Reading that stuff taught me a surprising amount about how to get away with crime. For instance, most of the clues that cops need for proving a murder in court come from finding the place where you killed the guy; after that comes whatever stuff they find on the body. Barring some fluke of chance, I didn't have a thing to worry about.

I slept through most of the day after the flood. Toward evening the dogs woke me. At least one but probably both of them had shat in my kitchen. For the second time they watched me clean the floor. They had worms, I learned.

The dog-shit smell covered up any stench lingering in my kitchen from when I'd punctured Wayne's stomach. I took the dogs out into the yard. The waters had receded, leaving upon the low parts of the houses and the fence a coat of scum that the sun must have baked dry while I slept. The grass had contorted into knotted clusters. The ground itself looked like the algae and silt at the bottom after a pond goes dry.

Both dogs seemed much livelier, just from a couple of meals. Useless showed the more mature personality. He stayed by me and walked where I walked. Stupid ran around the yard, sniffing at the swamp odors.

When I just glimpsed it out of the corner of my eye, I thought someone had painted a hex on the side of the garage, at the exact spot where I had killed Wayne. A hex, like they put on barns.

I looked at it again, and now it seemed to me that someone had hurled an open can of motor oil at the wall. Yet the closer I came to the mark, the less black it looked. From a few feet away I could see that Wayne's blood had sprayed there. I hadn't noticed while fishing his head out of the water during the blackout.

The sunny day had dried his blood dark on the yellow paint. The wooden brush I had used to scrub my apartment took the stain off with no trace, without even using ammonia.

Somewhere years ago I read how one of the detective's advantages is that committing a crime makes people superstitious. A criminal wants so badly not to get caught that often he invents bizarre reasons why he won't, rather than take sensible precautions. I'm not saying I got *that* crazy, but I definitely felt good about finding Wayne's blood. If all I needed to fear was some tiny fluke of chance that no one could predict, this stain had to be my fluke. And I'd caught it.

# 8

THE SET OF PAPERS THAT I KNEW I COULD USE were in the name Louis Collins. Pierre would have let me start work even if I hadn't brought them, because flood damage drove a ton of customers into the hardware store that Wednesday. We even ran out of a few items, so I got to see how the stockroom worked.

Pierre was happy with my work. He ordered sandwiches for Freddy and me. It was the first time I ever tasted fried catfish. While we ate in the stockroom Edith took a break from the register and joined us.

"Why do they call you Whitey?" she asked me. "Usually that's a nickname for someone with light blond hair."

"My hair was blond until I was sixteen," I lied.

"You're kidding," she said. "It just changed?"

I nodded. "That's not so strange."

"He's right," Freddy told her. "Both my brothers went from blond to brown when they grew up. It can be like overnight, practically."

Edith whistled. I couldn't shake the feeling she smelled something crooked about me. A little while later she asked, "So what's Michigan like?"

I shrugged. "It's flat and cold," I said. "Boring."

For a moment she studied my face, and I sussed just in time that she would closely watch my reaction to what she said next:

"Wait, you said the other day you come from Wisconsin."

"Sure do," I said, and paid attention to my sandwich.

In a minute or two she returned to the register. Freddy didn't seem to have noticed her trying to trap me in a lie, so I supposed she behaved that way toward everyone.

Later in the afternoon, business actually lulled. For a few minutes we had no customers at all in the store. I went up front to see if Pierre wanted me to punch out.

"So tell me," Edith said as I passed the register. "What kind of money do they use in Australia?"

"I still have some," I said. "I can bring it in if I think of it."

"What are they, pounds? Like in England?"

I shook my head. "I'll show you. Wait till I bring the money in." Quickly I walked away. I found Pierre and he sent me home. When I left, Edith had a smirk on her face.

I bought three pounds of crawfish on the way home. As soon as I opened my door Stupid jumped up to put his forepaws on me. A few steps behind him Useless waited for me to finish greeting the younger dog. I fed them. When I looked out my window I saw a light on in Christine's kitchen, so while the dogs ate I walked over to visit Christine.

She was in the front room of her house. The flood had leaked in under her front door and ruined the rug and some books.

"You feel like eating any crawfish?" I asked.

She shook her head, and spoke without taking her eyes from the damaged floor. "I fucking hate crawfish. I don't see what the big fucking deal about that shit is. Gumbo, too, and jambalaya. Leave that shit for the Cajuns."

I nodded as I watched her. She sat on the couch and ran her hands through her hair. It would never occur to her that I had any idea what she really had on her mind, and I couldn't tell her I knew. The thing in the freezer that Wayne had come to retrieve was a huge package of cocaine.

So she came home to find this coke missing from her freezer. Probably she also found signs around the place that Wayne had come by. If she'd just told me that, I would have pointed out how he must have thought that during the blackout the stuff would melt or go bad. I could have made her feel better, at least for a while, if she'd opened up to me.

Instead she got cranky. Cocaine isn't truly addictive, but you wouldn't ever believe that from watching coke fiends who can't get any. One time this guy who actually smuggled cash into the observation ward by hiding it up his ass paid an orderly to score for him, and then freaked out when the orderly just pocketed the money. The orderly even came the next day to say he'd spent it on coke. The guy tried to attack him.

So Christine became irritable. After a few minutes of her saying things under her breath and refusing to repeat them, I went home to eat. I decided to wait a few days before I told her about the dogs. The radio lulled me to sleep early that night.

The next day I didn't have to work at the hardware store until one in the afternoon, so in the morning I walked the dogs a few miles down Esplanade Avenue to a vet on Rampart Street. The vet took us without an appointment. He gave both dogs a shot to worm them and told me to start Useless on heartworm medicine. Stupid needed drops for his eyes. Otherwise, the dogs looked healthy. Of course I paid cash. Before I left, his receptionist gave me a form to fill out, so I made up a name and address.

After our long walk home I had just enough time to eat a shrimp sandwich from the seafood place. As soon as I walked into the hardware store, Edith said, "Did you bring in that money?"

"What money?" I asked, wondering what I owed her.

"From Australia," she said.

"Oh," I said. "No, you know? I forgot. I'm sorry. I have to look for it."

She nodded. "How come your shirt says Mike today?"

I walked to the stockroom as I answered, "This one I bought in a Goodwill store. I used to have to change the oil on lawnmowers." That was true.

She said something else, probably sarcastic. I ignored her. Inside the stockroom I found Pierre standing next to a loaded skiff. "Where you at, Whitey?" he said.

The clock said five to one. "I'm on time."

"No, 'where you at' means 'how are you.'"

"I'm okay," I told him.

"That's a New Orleans expression," Pierre explained. "You ain't lived down here too long, huh?"

"Not that long, no," I said. "Not yet."

"Well, look, I got to go do some errands," he said. "It's been quiet all morning, so I don't think you got to worry much. Just unload this stuff." He pointed at the skiff. "Most of it goes here in the stockroom. If you can't tell where something goes, leave it for me. I'll be back around five, in case we get people coming in for stuff on their way home from work.

"It's like that," he went on. "The day after a storm you get the people doing big repairs themselves, who just want to save money. Then for a week these other guys come in around dinner time for the smaller jobs, and they actually spend more."

Pierre strutted out of the back door and I began stocking. After a few minutes the buzzer sounded, so I went out front. I expected Edith to have a customer at the counter who needed help. She didn't.

"Is Pierre back there with you?" she asked.

"No," I said. "He said he had errands."

"Where'd he go?"

I shrugged.

"No, I mean, did he leave out the back door? Just like that?"

"Yeah," I told her, and waved one hand at the rear of the store. "He gave me a bunch of work to do back there."

Edith frowned at the front windows. "All right," she said. I went back to the stockroom.

A good while later, I carried an armload of caulk guns out to put on the shelves, and I saw a woman standing at the register.

"I'm sorry, Ma'am," I said. "I'll be with you in just a second."

"No, that's all right, baby," the woman said, smiling at me. "I'm just here seeing Edith."

"Yeah, this is my friend Marie," Edith said, sullenly.

As I went to the aisle where the caulk guns belonged, Marie resumed speaking, her voice soft enough that I could only make out the first few words she said: "So, anyways, you gotta tell him..." I didn't try to listen. But Edith went on with her voice the same volume, as if she and Marie were chatting in her living room.

One thing I heard Edith say was, "Whatever it is she does, it must be all kinds of wonderful, to make him this stupid."

Marie laughed.

"No, really," Edith said. "He's acting stupid, a man his age."

I didn't want to know what she was talking about. The next few hours I spent in the stockroom, until customers began coming in around dinner time, just as Pierre had predicted. He didn't come back to help me handle them, though.

The last customer left at a quarter after seven. Edith's usual smirk had grown angry, her eyes razor-sharp. At first I expected her to try the twenty-questions game on me again, yet as I restocked boxes of screws she only said, "Thanks, Whitey, you did all right." She crumpled a receipt from the register, flung it into the trash, and leaned against the wall, glaring at the floor, her arms folded.

Around twenty of eight, Pierre came in. "Hey, Whitey," he said.

"Hi," I said.

"Listen, let's go over what you need to do when you close up," he said. "Go break down them boxes in the stockroom. I'll be back there in a minute."

I crushed all the cartons I had emptied from the skiff. I carted them out the rear door and stuffed them into the dumpster in the parking lot. When I came back in, Pierre still hadn't come into the stockroom, so I went into the front. He was arguing with Edith.

They both turned to look at me when I said, "I put all the boxes into the dumpster."

"All right, man," Pierre said. "You go ahead and punch out. We'll show you how to lock up tomorrow."

"I don't work tomorrow," I said.

"Well, next time," he said. "Whichever is the next day you work at night, we'll show you then. I have a few things around here to do tonight."

Edith stayed quiet while I left.

A back counter in the seafood place sold Chinese food. I bought something I hadn't heard of called yacca mein and some egg rolls.

Then I got home. One or both of the dogs had shat worms on the kitchen floor, and some of the worms weren't dead yet.

After cleaning that up, I didn't feel like eating. So I went to Christine's. I brought my new handcuffs in my shirt pocket.

# 9

I MEANT TO GIVE CHRISTINE THE HANDCUFFS so she could wear them. Girls who dress in black wear handcuffs as jewelry on their belt or jacket. Christine had a leather motorcycle jacket hanging from a hook in her bedroom.

But I forgot all about giving her any presents when she opened her front door. It surprised her to see me, and it didn't make her smile. She didn't unlock the iron gate. "What do you want?" she asked.

"I just wondered what you were doing," I said.

"I'm fine. I was expecting someone else." She glanced up and down the street.

"So, you want to be alone?" I said.

Very quickly she drew a breath and let it out. "Whatever. Yeah." She closed the door.

That hurt my feelings, at first, I admit. As I walked back home around the block, it did piss me off. But I didn't get angry. Or if I did, I forgot about it while I peered in the windows of Cody's bar.

When he'd told me he only opened the place once a year, I don't think I really believed him. Yet here it was, locked up and dark, stools upside-down on top of the bar. The grandstand across the street at the track probably had a bar that opened whenever the horses ran, so the races brought Cody no business. Why he would pay for a liquor license just to open two weekends every May, I couldn't imagine. Maybe Alva paid for it, since I'm pretty sure she owned the building.

Two black men in a hatchback watched me walk toward my house. When they drove away I saw that they'd tied their car's back door closed with a rope. As I passed Pat's door, I thought about Alva, and I wondered why she let Christine run the rental properties for her. Maybe Alva just couldn't sell the houses and didn't want to bother with it, especially since she lived in Texas now, so Christine was the best she could do.

For a minute I stood with my hand on my doorknob. Inside I could hear the dogs scamper across the linoleum, eager to see me. In silence I studied the rear of Christine's house. It dawned on me that the "somebody else" she'd expected to find at her door instead of me must be a coke dealer. And all at once I thought of Cody and everybody else calling Christine their friend while they let her ruin herself.

A plan must have formed in my head, because I watched myself cross the yard to her house as though it were a movie.

By the time I reached Christine's I was running. Had she locked the gate over her back door, so that I would have had to fetch the key from under the stairs to open it, it would have broken my momentum. I might have stopped and thought about what I was doing.

Instead my hand yanked the gate aside and then the door opened and the kitchen flew past me, followed by Christine's bedroom. Dead ahead in the living room she stood watching me rush at her. She didn't look scared.

She began to say, "What are you doing?"

My arms wrapped around Christine, pinning her hands at her sides. It startled her. She fought a little bit, I think, but only on reflex, kicking the air.

The barrier between my hands and me fell away. A dirty warmth flooded across me. My sight failed. Now I couldn't see what my hands did, because they ruled me. I became my hands.

This daze burned away suddenly, and I found myself standing alone in the dark, losing balance. I stumbled over something on the floor. Time seemed to hold still. My stupor could only have lasted half a second, though, because what had snapped me awake was Christine's shout of pain.

The reason I was now in the dark was that I was in the bedroom with the door shut. The thing on the floor tripping my feet was Christine's leather jacket.

I flicked on the light.

Christine hung by her cuffed wrists from the coathook mounted on the top of the bedroom door, her back facing me. Her feet did not reach the floor.

That's a pretty strong coathook. The cheap aluminum kind we sold at the store would have snapped, easily. This one was brass.

I dislike violence. It never helps anything.

When you train a dog, for instance, you can't get frustrated. Anytime you lose your temper, any time you let anger into your voice, the dog can't learn what you're teaching him because he can't tell what made you mad.

I suspect that Useless's owner actually trained him somewhat, which also makes me think Useless may have gotten lost rather than abandoned. Stupid, on the other hand, had no idea how to sit or lie down on command.

After they've lived on the street a little while dogs become hard to teach, at least until they eat right long enough to get healthy. Actually I don't believe dogs can live on the street more than a short time because the garbage they eat there doesn't nourish them. They're not like cats, who can hunt. (For some reason, chows can survive, probably because they kill and eat feral cats.) It takes about a week for an adopted stray to straighten out and stop raiding the kitchen trash. During that time, hitting him has no effect other than causing pain.

In fact, you should never hit your dog at all other than giving him a light but firm tap on the snout. You need not raise your forearm whatsoever; all the force you need will come from your wrist. Smacking him harder than that can injure your dog, and even if it doesn't, the blow will set his head reeling. He can't learn that way.

Small rewards work even better, but it's easy to spoil him. Soon he won't eat unless you give him cold cuts or whatever. If you love a dog, you have to let him know who's boss.

❀ ❀ ❀

The steel cuffs dug into Christine's wrists. It hurt so much she couldn't yelp more than once. Instead she sucked air into her mouth around her clenched teeth, as though something hot had spilled on her hands.

I grabbed her around the waist and lifted her, to take the weight of her body off the cuffs.

"What the *fuck* is wrong with you?" she asked me.

I couldn't answer.

"Put me on the fucking floor!" she said, very loud. "Take these off!"

Without pulling her free I let go of her. The chain pulled taut, and once again her own body weight drove the cuffs into her flesh. The way her gasp muted into a whimper almost made me pick her back up. She couldn't believe how badly her wrists hurt. For just a moment I came very close to letting her off the hook.

On the floor next to her bed she kept her phone books. For some reason she had two copies of the Yellow Pages. I snatched them both plus the regular directory and placed all three beneath Christine's feet.

"What are you *doing*? Get me down!"

There atop the books she arched onto her toes so she could slide the chain off the brass hook. The hook had an ornamental barb on its cusp, though, and before she could get the chain over the barb I tugged one of the Yellow Pages out from under her. She panicked for just a flash as her footing tottered.

The chain couldn't slide now. Two phone books put Christine at exactly the correct height.

I still didn't have anything to say to her, a fact she at last seemed to grasp. Her breathing sounded pained to me, maybe because the sight of her arms stretched so high above her head suggested a whipping post. The surge of my own breath drowned out hers. I didn't like the way I found myself feeling. She was giving me urges.

The doorbell rang.

Christine almost managed to shout before I clasped my hand over her mouth. Her front teeth sank into a tiny fold of flesh at the base of my ring finger. Too late she thought to try and kick her heel backwards at my crotch.

The doorbell rang again. Her teeth let go of my skin and she screamed into my hand.

"That's not your friend," I whispered to her.

She screamed harder. My bitten hand didn't hurt much, especially because of my urges.

"That isn't your friend, out there," I told her again. "People who give you that shit aren't your friends."

Her scream tapered off, and she desperately sucked in air through her nose. My hand felt wet. I couldn't see her face to check whether she was crying.

"I'm your friend," I said.

She nodded her head, very slowly.

For some minutes we held still like that. The doorbell rang once more. We barely noticed. I splayed my fingers, just slightly at first, to let her breathe through her mouth.

Eventually she said, calmly, "You know, if Wayne comes here and finds me like this, he'll shoot us both."

"He won't come," I promised.

Right away I knew I shouldn't have said that. I took my hand from her mouth and examined the fresh tiny mark her teeth had left on my ring finger. It bled when I spread my hand open to study it.

She looked over her shoulder at me and asked, "How do you know he won't?"

I ignored her, pretending she had really hurt my hand. I just needed an excuse so I could be alone for a few minutes, to let me think clearly. "Do you have peroxide?" I asked her.

She shook her head.

"Then I have to go to my house," I said, checking around the room so I wouldn't have to look at her. "What do want in your mouth?"

"Excuse me?" she said.

"I have to gag you," I said. "What do you want me to put in your mouth to keep you from yelling?"

Very politely she said, "Usually in a situation like this, you would use the woman's underwear to gag her."

"Okay," I said, and walked over to her dresser. "Which drawer?"

"I meant the ones I have on."

All at once I saw she was making fun of me, or playing some trick to turn the tables. I played along. I wouldn't have done so normally, but those urges make me act crass, which is why I've never liked them. I reached under her skirt and tried to yank her underpants down.

She cried out as if I had hurt her, so I let go. "Easy," she told me. "Lift my skirt up first, and slide them off me slowly."

I did it the way she wanted. A thought fired through my mind that I might get upset, but other ideas distracted me from it.

"So," I said, holding her underpants.

"Are they dirty?"

"I don't know," I said. I mean, I wasn't going to look.

"Smell them," she told me.

I tried to say, "What?"

All I could see over Christine's shoulder were her eyes. "Smell them," she said again. "Smell the inside. Hold them against your face."

And I did it. For a long time. I started liking it.

"You know what?" Christine said. "My shoulders hurt. I sure would love to have that other phone book under my feet again. I wouldn't try to get loose this time. If you let me have the other phone book, I'll do anything you want me to."

I squeezed my eyes shut.

"Although," she added, "I guess I'll probably be doing whatever you want, anyway. But if I was up a bit higher, I could stick my ass out better."

Which was not what I wanted to hear. I've never been able to stand anyone who uses sex that way, and I've been around some very sick people. Christine thought she could just start calling the shots once she showed me her privates. I had a real struggle remembering that she wasn't in control of herself.

# 10

Two days later, when I went back to the hardware store, my mind wouldn't stay at work. Every time a police car passed by on the street my heart sank into my stomach. To make it worse, Edith started on me the moment I walked in the door.

"How you doing, Whitey?" she said. "You bring that money today?"

Again I didn't remember at first what she meant. Then I just decided to put that whole ruse to bed, since she wasn't going to forget it like a normal person would. "No, you know what?" I said. "I can't find it. I looked for that stuff. I know I had it when I got here, but it's gone. I think someone might have borrowed it."

"Borrowed it for what?" she asked, smiling.

"I don't know, I just don't have it anymore," I said. She said something else, but I walked to the stockroom with a sour face and one hand clenching my stomach.

"Where you at, Whitey?" Pierre said.

"Not too good," I told him.

"Stomach bothering you?"

I nodded.

"You could work, though?" Pierre asked me. "If you need to go home early or something, just say so."

"I think I can work," I said. "If it gets worse, I'll tell you."

So they excused my acting slightly distraught. The day crawled past. Customers came in, but not enough of them to keep me from thinking about what awaited me at home after work. I wished I had four or five skiffs to unload in the stockroom.

That day I noticed how Edith only picked on me until Pierre left. It had been that way the last time I'd worked, too; once he was out of the building, Edith backed off. She didn't talk to me other than to call for prices as she rang customers. As soon as Pierre went out the door she became reserved, even pensive.

And again he didn't come back when he said he would. This time he showed up by six, and Edith didn't say anything about it. Neither Pierre nor I wanted to be near her, though, so whenever we didn't have actual customers to help, Pierre took me in the stockroom to teach me how to close up after an evening shift.

At one point he asked me if I'd ever crossed the Causeway, which was a twenty-four-mile bridge over a lake if you come to New Orleans from that direction.

"I'm not sure," I told him.

"The lake?" he said, not believing I didn't know what he meant. "Lake Ponchartrain? You have to know if you saw that."

"I came over a lot of water getting here," I said, "but I don't know. I drove here at night, for one thing."

Pierre started describing this resort park that had closed down on the lake. His aunt had gotten married at this place when he was a kid. He mentioned that only white people were allowed there, and remembering this fact either embarrassed or saddened him.

To keep from having to act normal around his wife while she brooded, he would talk about anything, and for that same reason, I would listen.

Pierre even kept me there ten minutes past the normal clockout time, until eight-forty. Then he said, "Well, all right, Whitey, I think you're set to close by yourself tomorrow night. We'll see how you do."

"All right," I agreed. "Sounds good."

I punched out and left. At the front door I said good night to Edith, and she just nodded at me without looking up from whatever printed matter she held in her hands.

Outside I watched traffic while I made up my mind whether or not to buy Chinese food. It would still taste good, no matter how long everything took me until I got a chance to eat. Chinese food's never a foolish investment.

But I couldn't see myself waiting at the counter, knowing what I knew, even though by that point everything had to be all right. So I walked up Gentilly Boulevard.

First I went to my house and fed Stupid and Useless. I had to clean their shit off the kitchen floor, too. Then I brought them out to the yard for a run. Stupid bounded away a little, but for the most part dogs who've lived on the street recently find the outdoors unexciting.

Stupid liked running for sticks, though of course he would bring them only partway back to me and then settle down to gnaw them. Useless felt no inclination to join the game. He stayed near me and only walked when I did.

Across the yard Christine's house waited for me. That morning I had closed all her shutters before leaving, and now the windowless walls made me wonder how anyone could see this building and not know it was a prison.

I put the dogs back inside my house.

On my keyring I now carried both copies of each of the four keys to Christine's. Next to them I also had the key to the handcuffs.

As I unlocked her back gate and quietly swung it open, the gate itself felt flimsy to me. The wooden door actually had more heft. And I knew that wasn't the case with the wooden door in the front, where it made much more difference because even if she didn't pry the front gate off, she could shout to passersby, maybe even flag down drivers on Gentilly.

But if that had happened, the cops would have come for me at the store. I had told her where I worked. Even if she didn't know the exact name, Pierre's was the nearest hardware store to her house.

The lock on the back door clacked very loudly when I turned the key. Trying to sneak up on Christine wouldn't work, at least not this time.

I found her in her living room, lying on the couch with a cigarette in her mouth and the television on.

"When do you feed me?" she asked. I could see the smirk hiding at the edges of her face.

"Are you hungry now?" I said.

She nodded. "I want Chinese food." I told her about the seafood store. She said, "No, I want it from a real Chinese place. Plus, that store closed at nine." Instead she told me to call a place on Carrollton and have them deliver.

To use the phone I had to unlock the front door—just the wooden one, so I could reach through the gate and grab the phone cord out of her mailbox. Some mail had come, too, three letters that looked like bills. I brought all of it inside. From her kitchen Christine got the menu for the other restaurant and I ordered dumplings and fried rice for us.

When I hung up I said, "He says it'll be here in forty minutes."

Christine nodded faintly, staring at me.

Right away I could feel her effect on my body. I don't just submit to urges; it takes me a while to decide if and how I want to react. Having left the house earlier to go to work broke some kind of spell she had worked on me for the past two days. Now it would gradually take effect again, if I let it.

The closeness of her I liked. The part I didn't like, in truth, wasn't her fault. She just had something wrong with her that made her want to perform immoral, unhealthy acts. What bothered me was how I participated in it. These practices that she liked—not that I'd had any time with anyone else so I could compare it—these practices were depraved, in a lot of ways. Since I wasn't the one with the drug habit, I had a responsibility to control myself. She might upset me and something bad might happen.

And I knew all that, but still I wanted to do it with her. All day at the store, even while I worried about the cops arriving to take me away, certain moments from the past two days kept flickering in my head. She kept things at the back of her closet shelf, toys you see in raunchy magazines, and she made me use them on her. The sight of it kept coming back to me.

So now I sat there, staring back at her, feeling physical signs of wanting. I had always imagined an act of sex would require too much concentration, but the arousal came unbidden, unaided. Given time, it would begin to feel good. Or I would begin to think it did.

"I was bad today," she whispered to me.

"What did you do bad?"

"Does it matter?" Christine said, pouting a little. "If you love me, you want to make me behave myself. Right?"

Going without coke made her act this way. It's not a real withdrawal, actually, because cocaine isn't technically addictive. The drug changes your brain chemistry, though. So I shouldn't have done any of this stuff with her. I should have stayed stronger.

Not that I didn't have a good time.

# 11

THE NEXT NIGHT I CLOSED THE STORE BY MYSELF. Of course, Edith had to be there too, since I couldn't touch the register. Pierre took off around five, saying he would go home and take a nap.

A minute after he left, while I placed screws and bolts into their tiny plastic drawers in the fastener aisle, I overheard Edith talking on the phone. I only paid attention because we were alone in the store and I thought at first she was speaking to me.

"Pierre, it's me," she said. "As soon as you get this, call me at the store. I need to ask you something."

From time to time I peeked around the corner of the aisle. Edith leaned against the register, staring at a stain on the floor near the front door, her lips pursed and her eyes still, as if watching some awful story on the news. The way her eyebrows trembled a little every few seconds told me she didn't really feel as angry as she tried to look.

When I finished with the screws and bolts, I actually went to the register to start a conversation with her.

"Who are these girls?" I asked, pointing at some photographs she kept taped to the wall beside the register.

She blinked at me for a few seconds, then she said, "Those are my nieces." Pointing at a picture of three girls together, Edith recited their names. "Eileen, Jennifer, and Laura. They're my sister's girls."

The middle one had braces and long hair. "Boy, she's sure good-looking," I said.

"Yeah, that's Jennifer," Edith said. "She's a model."

"Is she really? What does she model for?"

Edith named some catalogs and department stores, none that I had heard of. Mostly I worried whether she knew I was only asking so we could have something to talk about. If she did suspect that, she let it slide and kept talking.

"She don't like her braces," Edith said. "She wants the kind that you can't see."

I hadn't heard about them.

"Yeah, they make them out of..." Edith rolled her eyes at the ceiling, as if recalling who sang her favorite song when she was in eighth grade. Then she shook her head and said, "I don't know. It's fiberglass, maybe. But you can't see them. And her father insisted she get the old-fashioned kind. She threw some fit, I'll tell you."

I laughed. "Did she?"

Edith chuckled, too. "Yeah, you right. She called me up, going, 'Aunt Edith, can I come live with you?' She doesn't talk to her father no more. This is two months already. Oh, she's mad." She laughed louder.

Even though she could be nosy, I liked Edith. I didn't mean for what happened to her to happen. But that came later.

Pierre never called her back. After we locked the gate over the front of the store, Edith offered me a ride. I said no thanks. It didn't make sense for me to have anyone at the store know where I lived. I told her I just felt like walking. She kept her eyes on me until I walked away.

I bought a bag of shrimp and went home. Once again I had to clean shit off the kitchen floor, but there wasn't much of it. I fed the dogs. They finished quickly. Stupid sat at command beside my chair, his eyes locked on each shrimp I ate. Dogs can't have seafood, though. Useless knew better than to even ask. He lay on the floor near the back door. As we all sat there, I realized I hadn't owned a dog in twenty years. Thinking about it almost made me cry.

Something profound passes between a person and his dog. Listen to the way dog owners in public speak to their dogs; they chide them like children, complain about injustices the animal could in no way have caused. A dog turns into a family member when you adopt it.

When I finished I took them out in the yard. They ran a bit more now, especially Stupid. I had the next day off, and I wanted to spend most of it out in the yard with the dogs. I still hadn't resumed work on the fence after the flood.

I picked up a stick for Stupid to fetch. He leaped to snatch it from my hand, so I waved the stick in the air. On his second jump he grabbed it. For the first time I could see how powerful a dog Stupid was, despite his stunted growth from living on the street. Now that he had the confidence that somebody loved him, this dog played rough. The vet had agreed that one of Stupid's parents was an American Staffordshire Terrier, which is a fancy name for a pit bull.

"That's a tough fucking dog," Pat said from the alley. I hadn't heard him come out.

"He isn't dangerous," I said.

"Sure, he is," Pat said. "You want him dangerous. Clamp those jaws on some burglar's ass, guy'll never walk again. That's a good dog. Probably a fighting dog, isn't it?"

"I don't know. I just found them both," I told Pat. "I'll make sure they won't be any trouble."

"I ain't worried about it," Pat said. "It's good to have a watchdog. I used to have a really good German shepherd."

We talked awhile. He told me about dog fighting, which I had never heard of. Pit bulls have really strong jaws and don't let go when they bite, so they're popular for this sport. Men gamble on it. The dogs tear each other to pieces until one of them's dead.

Maybe Pat saw that the topic bothered me, or maybe he had something to do inside, but he left. Stupid kept his jaws locked on the stick so tightly that I lifted him off the ground and swung him in a circle around me. The stick broke, and he landed in a heap on the grass.

We played like that for half an hour before I put the dogs back inside. Then I went over to Christine's.

Acting on the urges regularly made me cocky about them. I went into her house through the back door, turning over plans in my head about what I felt like doing with her. I took my handcuffs out of my pocket as I went from the kitchen through the bedroom.

Christine lay on her couch, watching television. I walked directly to her, locked the cuffs on her wrists, and pulled her upright by the chain. She smiled as I led her to the front door. No other hooklike object suggested itself, so I bent her over with the cuffs looped on the doorknob.

I reached under her skirt for her underwear, only to find none. I dropped my pants to my ankles and opened her shirt.

"Tough day at the office, dear?" she said, and laughed.

We got started pretty quick. I don't know how long we'd been at it when someone outside knocked on the door.

Instantly she stood up, and I stumbled backwards, trying to cover my privates while yanking up my pants. I couldn't tell whether whoever was outside had heard us doing it.

Christine called through the door, "Hello? Who is it?"

"It's the police, ma'am," a man answered.

Her eyes met mine and widened. "Okay," she said. "Can you wait just a second? I'm real sorry."

She held her hands out to me. It took a second before I understood she wanted me to unlock the cuffs. I fumbled with the key a little, too. When both cuffs were off, she handed them to me. Then she took a set of keys from beside her television and unlocked the front door.

One policeman stood outside, wearing a suit. He was black and younger than I. He introduced himself calmly, but I didn't even notice his name.

Instead I stared dumbfounded at the keys in Christine's hand. She'd had another set all this time and just left them out where I could find them. Was this whole thing a joke to her?

The policeman asked if he could talk to Christine alone.

# 12

I WENT TO MY HOUSE AND GOT WAYNE'S GUN. It was a black revolver with a little picture of a lion engraved in the handgrip.

As I came back across the yard carrying the gun I made a conscious effort not to get frantic. When I got to Christine's house I realized I still hadn't opened her shutters. There was no way I could spy on her while she talked to the cop.

Everything in the yard lay still. Outside on Gentilly cars passed. The shadow cast by the fence hid me from the street lamps. In a tree beside the neighbor's house a bird hopped forward from its sleeping place onto a slim branch to watch me, and its neck stretched and recoiled in time with the branch's bobbing, so that the bird's head stayed in the same place.

What with my job at the hardware store and spending every night at Christine's, I had not resumed repairing the fence since the storm, so I had not worked my way to this section yet. Of the five houses that shared the yard, only two faced Gentilly Boulevard: Christine's and her next-door neighbor's. Their houses were not exactly parallel, but would have formed a V had both buildings extended back far enough. The fence that ran between them was in fact a two-piece gate, twenty or twenty-five feet long, with dolly wheels on its bottom. Until now I had not noticed the wheels. Since it was nighttime I could not see the fence well, but obviously no one had swung it open in a long time. Apart from the gated driveway on the other side of Christine's house this was the only entrance big enough to admit a vehicle into the yard. For some reason it seemed designed for horse carriages rather than cars.

After a short while I felt calm, and I walked back across the yard to my house. The dogs watched me put the gun back under my bed. Then I stood at my window, watching the yard.

I hadn't met the neighbor who lived by the bird tree, in the house next to Christine's. The night she'd shot coke in front of me she'd started to tell me something about the old man who lived there, that he caused problems by complaining to Alva. Christine had left the story half finished, though.

The moon hung strange in the sky. Here, closer to the equator, the moon traveled more quickly across the heavens, and even shone bigger overhead, but this night something else affected it. I stared, I don't know for how long.

Then I touched something loose on the windowsill. It was the missing third shelf track, the one ripped out of the wall by my bed. Until just then I hadn't noticed it on the sill because it matched the metal frame. This shelf track weighed more than I expected, because I was used to the aluminum kind we sold in the store. Obviously, the previous tenant had used this one to prop open the window. It was about two feet long.

That's one detail I noticed about New Orleans: Every house has some hat rack or ornamental hamper taken down and left in a drawer or closet, in case some future tenant should care to remount the thing.

Movement in the yard caught my eye. Christine came out her back door and shut its iron gate behind her. For some reason she had changed clothes into a long dress that she used as a nightgown, the color of white lace that hasn't been washed in a long time. The moonlight made her glow, and I couldn't tell where the fabric ended and her skin began. The bottom of the dress swung about her bare feet as she crossed the grass.

In the back of my mind I wondered if the dogs had left any droppings there. If she stepped in some it would've really ruined the moment.

When she had almost reached my back door I remembered that she didn't know about Stupid and Useless yet. So I hurried back outside to meet her.

"Can I come in?" she asked.

"Let's go to your house," I said.

Christine brushed a strand of hair away from her eyes and said, "All right." I picked her up and carried her back across the grass. She didn't weigh much. As I walked she tucked her face into my throat. At her back door she swung her feet down onto the steps and led me inside.

When we got to her bedroom she spoke again. "I need to not play the game tonight," she said.

"What's wrong?" I asked, not only because I wanted to know but because I didn't want her to see me react to the word *game*.

Christine shook her head. I sat on her bed with her on my lap facing away from me. After a short while I could feel her weeping. I asked what was wrong a few more times.

Finally she whispered, "Wayne's dead."

A sound came out of my mouth. I pretended to clear my throat. "What happened?" I asked her.

She buried her face in my shirt and wouldn't answer.

"What happened to him?" I asked again. "Why did the cops come to tell you that?"

We sat still for few minutes, and then she said, "Someone killed him. One of his cop friends knew he used to come here, so that detective wanted to know when I'd seen him last."

I nodded, to keep her talking while I came up with some questions to ask. I needed to drum into her mind that I knew nothing about Wayne unless she told me.

"His car was parked up the street," she said. "They killed him the night of the flood, and his car was parked where the edge of the water was. Like he was coming here."

"Why come here in the flood?"

"Probably he came to check on me," she said. "When I wasn't here, he must have went back and they got him between here and his car."

"Did someone shoot him, or something?" I asked.

She shook her head. "I don't want to talk about it."

We didn't. Instead we sat there in the dark. For a while she cried more, then we started kissing and it led to sex. When you have sex regularly, it can seem different than usual. That's how it felt right then. We did it a gentle way, with me lying on my back and her sitting on me.

When we finished she lay beside me and lit a cigarette. I've never smoked, but it looked very satisfying. We lay still.

Out of the blue she said softly, "I've been wanting to ask you something all week. Are you an asshole or a kook?"

Although I'd heard her clearly, I said, "What?"

"Every man who can make me come like that always turns out to be either an asshole or a kook," she explained. "I just thought I'd find out up front."

I had seen that expression in print, but I'd never heard it used in conversation before, so without realizing what she meant I asked, "Make you come where?"

Christine pulled a big drag on her cigarette and sighed. When she exhaled she said, "So you're a kook, then."

The next morning we woke up close to noon. I was glad I didn't have to work. We lounged in bed for half an hour until Christine got up to make coffee.

A short while later she brought in two cups and set one on the night-stand beside me. The other she kept in her hands as she sat cross-legged on the bed. She sipped it loudly.

"Are you still sad?" I asked. "About Wayne."

She turned toward me as if this were a stupid question. "Yeah," she said. "I'm still sad. He's *dead*."

"You have me now," I said.

Christine stared at me.

"I'll protect you," I told her.

A ring of ice melted in her heart when I said that, I could tell. She nodded and began paying attention to the window across the room. We stayed that way for some time, so quiet that I noticed the sound of cars passing outside on Gentilly. Normally when you live near constant traffic the noise becomes a background hum you don't hear anymore.

Soon I got out of bed and announced, "Today I'm going to work on the fence." While I stretched I added, "We should go to the lumberyard."

Christine mumbled, "Yeah."

A while later I went out her kitchen door. I glanced back into the house behind me and saw Christine still sitting on her bed, staring at the window that faced her driveway and the side of Cody's bar. This was the only window in her house that had no shutter. She could have opened it and climbed out at any time while I'd had her captive, so I must have known on some level that we were just playing.

Back in my apartment I brushed my teeth. Then I took the dogs with me out into the yard. As usual Stupid bounded back and forth and Useless followed me around. Much to my surprise, the older lawnmower started right up the first time I yanked the cord. Somebody must have maintained the thing properly for the seal on its gas tank to still be watertight. Both dogs darted away from the noise.

I killed the mower and wheeled it into the shed. Without fresh planks from the lumberyard there wasn't much I could do in the way of carpentry. Instead I decided on painting the long double gate between Christine's and her cranky neighbor's.

As I carried the paint and a roller from my house toward the gate, the thought struck me that I should unshutter Christine's windows. I laid the painting stuff on the grass and walked around her house, unfastening each set of shutters—three on this side, a small one for the bathroom on the back, and one on the other side facing the bar—except for the two on the front of her house, because the fence meant I'd have to walk through her house to reach them. Christine had the keys both to this gate and to the one across her driveway, and I didn't feel like asking her for them.

I discovered a small wooden bench next to Christine's living room window, right near where I'd hid in the shadows the night before. Somehow I had mowed the lawn without noticing this thing. Whoever had built the fence had nailed this bench together out of scraps left over from the job. It stood only as high as my knee. No one had ever painted it, so one corner of the seat curled upward where rain had warped it.

While I stirred the paint, Christine came out her back door and strolled around the corner to me. She had a banjo. As she walked she turned the little knobs that change the pitch of the strings.

"Where'd these dogs come from?" she asked.

"I found them," I said. "They'll make good watchdogs. Pat likes them."

She shrugged and kept tuning.

"I know you don't like dogs," I said. "I can put them in my house, if you want."

"I don't mind dogs," she said.

"Oh? Because you said you hated them."

"Whatever," Christine said. "As long as I don't have to clean up their shit, they're fine."

Whatever trance we had shared for the past several days, it had waned. The way we spoke to each other now was blunt and untouched by make-believe. It felt good. Even through her brusque self-attention I could sense some kind of respect I had gained in her eyes.

"I didn't know you played the banjo," I said.

"What you don't know about me," she said without looking up, "could fill the phone book." She sat on the bench.

First she made a few false starts. It must have been a long time since she'd played. By the time I was actually painting the gate, she had it back. When a song would change parts she might have to do it over to figure out the words or where her fingers should be pressing down the strings, but she could play. Her singing wavered and crackled as though parts of her voice had rusted away, yet it was still very pretty.

When I had finished painting the inside of the fence, I walked around to her back door and crossed through the house so I could open the shutters on the front windows. Christine stayed on the bench, plucking her banjo strings.

With the shutters thrown wide, sunlight flooded her living room. As I walked back through the house her phone started ringing. I paused for a moment, not sure why I did. From outside, she couldn't hear the phone. It rang three times, then her answering machine clicked on. Her recorded voice said, through the machine's tiny speaker, "I'm not home right now, leave a message."

The machine beeped, and then a man said, "Hello. This is Michael Ennis."

Michael, that was his name. When we were in homeroom together, his bus passes used to come with his name abbreviated "Mich," so we called him Michigan as a joke.

Ennis began by reminding Christine who he was. He asked her if by any chance she knew how to reach me, and he used my real name.

If I just erased that message, he might call back again when I wasn't here to intercept it. So I picked up the phone.

# 13

"What do you want?" I asked.

"My name's Michael Ennis," he said. "I'm trying to reach—"

"It's me, Ennis," I told him. "What do you want?"

"Oh, hey, man," Ennis said, and paused for just a breath, trying to read my voice. "I didn't expect *you* to answer," he said. "Are you... Something going on with you and that chick that rents the apartments out?"

"Yeah," I said. To keep from letting him know how badly it unnerved me to hear from him, I spoke as little as possible.

"Well, good for you, man. Outstanding." He paused. I pictured him scratching his jaw. "Listen, we need to talk."

"About what?"

"Look, I know about what happened," he said. When I didn't respond, he added, "With you, up here. You know?"

For a few seconds we both fell silent. It became obvious I had to say something. I said, "Yeah?"

"Uh-huh," Ennis said.

"What about it?"

"Well, do you have some time to talk right now?" he asked me.

"No," I said.

"I'll give you my number," he said. "Call me collect from a payphone somewhere. When's good for you? We need a few minutes to talk."

Once I'd written his number on my palm, I told him I'd call him in two hours. Then I told him not to call me at Christine's again, ever. He claimed he'd only called her as a long shot, hoping I'd taken his advice to look for an apartment in the neighborhood.

"I'm on your side," he said. "You know that, don't you?"

I assured him I did, and hung up, my heart pounding. Then I erased his message off Christine's machine. She had a really old machine, the kind that looks like a tape recorder, so it was easy to figure how it worked.

When I came back out to the yard, Useless lay at Christine's feet while she played. Stupid stood sniffing the wet paint.

"What's their names?" she asked, so I told her and she laughed. "I like this guy," she said, nodding at Useless.

I put another coat of paint on the gates. It took an hour, maybe. Listening as Christine's playing improved relaxed me a little, but my thoughts kept returning to Ennis. Inwardly I told myself over and over that he would have called the police on me already if he intended to call them at all. This thought failed to comfort me.

I wound up calling him from the bank of payphones outside the Circle K on Esplanade, forty minutes earlier than we'd agreed.

"Sorry I'm early," I said.

"No, that's all right," Ennis said. "How's everything down there?"

"Okay," I said.

"You know they're looking for you up here," he said.

"I know."

"All right, well," he said. "You should've told me when I saw you. You know? I didn't know anything about it. I could've said something to someone about seeing you down there, not knowing the situation, and you know how people talk."

"Sure do." I swallowed, eager to hide that I knew he had gone back home and inquired about me. It wasn't like some big dragnet had contacted him, hunting me down.

"I could've said something, somebody else repeats it—*boom!* You're fucked. That happens to people in your position every day."

"Honestly," I told him, "I knew I could trust you, Michael, but I didn't want to involve you in it."

"Cool. I understand," he said. "I just didn't want you worrying. You know, because I could've said something, or whatever. Not knowing."

"All right. Thanks, Michael."

Ennis cleared his throat. I could sense him willing the conversation forward.

"So," he said, "you doing all right for money?"

"Yeah." I glanced at the parking lot around me. No one was near enough to overhear me. "I work at a hardware store."

"Would you be up for making a little extra?" he said. "Doing me a favor. I'll make it worth your while."

This favor took him a long time to explain. Tara, the girl I'd seen with him outside the diner that morning, was a dancer at a men's club. (I took this news without comment.) Ennis had moved Tara down here and set her up in an apartment while she attended college, and then she dropped out and went back to stripping. Apparently Ennis took a great deal of heat from his wife over this whole episode. Just this past week Tara had stopped talking to Ennis altogether, and Ennis believed she had another man. Someone older, he guessed, with money.

"You ever been in love?" Ennis asked me.

"I am now," I answered. It worried me to hear these words come from my mouth.

He sighed. "So you know how it is, then. I'm very embarrassed at what I'm asking you."

And then at last he asked: Would I spy on Tara for him? First of all, he wanted to see her mail. She had it delivered to a post-office box at a station in the business district.

"I can't steal it from her post-office box," I said.

"You can if you have the key," he said. "That's in her apartment. That's real easy to get."

The whole time he described what he wanted me to do, I knew that I had to accept whatever terms he laid. It worked in my favor that he believed I was out of my mind. That kept him from getting too pushy. He thought he needed to talk to me as if I were falling for this "job" routine, as though he were recruiting a professional snoop rather than blackmailing me into becoming one. It left me some tiny room to maneuver. When they're chasing you, you have to stay ahead of them any way you can, even if it's just by inches.

Ennis sent the packet Express Mail, so I got it on Monday, the first piece of mail at my new address. Pat brought it back to me on his way out to the bar. I didn't like the idea that Pat had seen my real name, but as far as I could tell he didn't talk to Christine much, so it wouldn't matter.

Inside the cardboard envelope were two crude diagrams of Tara's apartment, one drawn as I would see it entering through her door and one drawn as seen from overhead, like a map. In both drawings Ennis had used arrows to show the jewelry case under which she kept the spare key to her PO box. On a third sheet of paper torn from the same spiral notebook he had also sent an eye-view drawing of the back of her house and a map of the entire property. The remaining item was a key to Tara's door, wrapped in a wad of tissue so it wouldn't tear through the edge of the cardboard mailer.

I had to work that night. There were no customers when I got to the store, so I asked Pierre to show me how to make keys.

"You don't know how to cut keys?" Edith asked. "I thought you worked in a hardware store in Wisconsin."

"It was my grandfather's store," I said. "He never showed me."

"It ain't complicated," Pierre said. The cutter was beside the register. He taught me how to work it, then had me practice by duplicating the keys to the store. I would need my own set in case I had to open the place for a morning shift.

The rest of the evening I spent stocking shelves, helping a few customers, and trying to keep away from Edith. Since Pierre stayed in the store all night, she was unpleasant again.

# 14

Tuesday evening I took Stupid's leash and walked to Esplanade to catch the bus downtown. It brought me to Canal Street. From there I took the streetcar up Saint Charles Avenue to Felicity Street. I got off in front of that diner where Ennis had spotted me my first day in town.

Tara's house was on Prytania Street, which ran parallel to Saint Charles a few blocks toward the river. The houses over here were bigger and much more ornate than the ones where I lived, but somehow this area struck me as less savory, maybe because I could tell wealthy people used to own these buildings and now the neighborhood had gone to seed.

A lot more white people lived here, or at least were walking around on the sidewalk. When I got to Tara's block, I approached an older man and woman chatting on a front porch and held my dog leash up for them to see.

"Excuse me," I said. "Did you folks happen to see a brown dog run by here?"

They looked at each other, as if conferring on their answer, then looked back at me and shook their heads.

"What'd it look like?" the man said. He didn't have many teeth.

"Like a Labrador," I told him, and put my hand just higher than my knee. "About this big."

They shook their heads again. "Uh-uh," the lady said. "Sure didn't."

"All right, thank you." I walked away.

"Hope you find him," the man called after me.

I walked farther down the block, checking in each yard and alley I passed. Another man came walking toward me, and when I asked if he'd seen a dog he just shook his head.

When I got to Tara's house I paused to stare down her driveway. The old people down the block still had their eyes on me. I tilted my head as if something in the back yard had caught my eye, then I walked down the driveway.

Tara lived in a large boarding house. Most of the homes in that part of town were built as single-family dwellings for rich people, but this one seemed designed for multiple tenants. For one thing, the back yard was a dirt parking lot. Also, different apartments had their doors facing out along an upper porch, exactly the way Ennis had drawn it for me except that there were four doors instead of three. I knew Tara's apartment number, though.

In case anyone in the house could see me, I scanned the yard for my imaginary dog. Tara's blue Toyota was gone. I walked up the steps to the porch and directly to Tara's door. Nothing moved anywhere. A sticker on her window said the premises were protected by an alarm company, but Ennis had told me the service hadn't been turned on for as long as she had lived here.

The trick to entering any locked room where you don't belong is to act as though you own the place. After two years or so of living in captivity you get good at that. That's why you read about these guys in prison who pull these amazing capers, stealing drugs from the infirmary or keys from a trustee's office or whatever, just by not hesitating when the chance comes to snatch stuff. If one of Tara's neighbors had suddenly appeared on the porch as I unlocked her door, I would've nodded a polite hello as if I had something else important on my mind.

Once I relocked her door behind me, though, my heart thumped so hard I could hear it out loud. I peeked out the window for anyone who might have seen me. My hands shook. I spent a long while calming myself—probably not as long as it seemed right then, but at least a minute, I'm sure. Finally I turned around.

I was in the wrong apartment.

It didn't look anything like Ennis's drawing.

Now panic hit me. Had a person emerged from the bathroom right then, wondering who I was, I would have gotten upset, no question.

But the apartment was empty. My blood stopped roaring in my ears, and I reasoned with myself: It couldn't be the wrong apartment. How could two apartments in the same house have the same key? That only happens with Japanese cars, so far as I've ever heard. Ennis hadn't said anything about this key's being a master key. He would have warned me.

Of course I'd left Ennis's diagrams back at my house. If I got caught and the cops searched me, my story about the lost dog would fall apart once they found maps and instructions in my pocket. But when I think clearly, my memory's very good, and I'd spent a lot of time studying his drawings. This was not the room he'd drawn.

First of all, the dresser where he claimed she kept her jewelry box was nowhere in sight. Instead a bed filled that part of the room. Over by the bathroom door was an antique vanity, like a makeup table you would see in an old-time actress's dressing room on a TV show.

Something about the bed drew my eye, and I realized that the headboard—a semicircle of black polished wood trimmed with a chrome rail—matched the drawing Ennis had sent me. For some reason he'd included this detail. That meant that this was the same bed in a different part of the room, and it dawned on me that Tara had moved her furniture around.

She'd gotten rid of her dresser.

I laid the dog leash on the carpet and went to the vanity. The jewelry box lay there by the mirror, so I picked it up and looked beneath it. No key.

This vanity looked expensive and old, yet it had no dust on it and the wood finish didn't match her bed. She must have bought it recently, I decided. The mirror had lots of those little bubble pocks inside the glass. Beside the jewelry box stood a tiny copper frame, three inches high, with a photograph in it of a girl sitting next to her grandmother at a picnic table. The girl was Tara.

In the wide drawer, the center one that would be right above her lap when she sat looking in the mirror, Tara had a bunch of makeup as well as business cards from six or seven men. I didn't touch any of it.

Tucked all the way to the back lay a manilla envelope, big enough to hold a magazine. I slid the envelope out and opened it. Inside it I found nine or ten photos and a few birthday cards. Tara was in some of the photos, but a small gray terrier was in all of them. I read the birthday cards, and they turned out not to be birthday cards at all but sympathy cards, the kind you would send someone whose grandfather died, only these cards were for a dog. I'd never seen anything like it.

It struck me that I'd forgotten about Tara's dog completely. I hadn't even asked Ennis about it.

I placed the pictures and cards back in the envelope and replaced the envelope exactly where I'd found it.

Either side of the vanity was a column of three drawers, each one half as wide but twice as deep as the center drawer. I opened them one at a time, careful not to disturb whatever she kept inside. In one drawer I found a stack of photographs, the big glossy kind that movie stars autograph to mail their fans. It was Tara with no shirt on, wearing a long blonde wig and squeezing her own breasts, pouting like a child. The picture was the same on each one, but they all had writing on them in black magic marker. The marker itself lay in the drawer beside the pictures.

On each photo she had written, "Love you, Daddy! XXX, Anisette."

In this stack she had maybe forty copies of this picture. I took five of them. I didn't have anything to carry them in, so I went into her kitchenette and got a plastic bag from beneath the sink. The photos fit in there fine, though you could sort of see them through the plastic.

Also under the sink, leaning against the back corner, stood a wooden rack for paper towels. Two folding metal fixtures and their screws lay beside it. On the wall by the sink two square patches of bare white marred by screwholes showed where this rack had once hung.

Tara didn't have a dishwasher, and a load of dishes sat dry in the sink rack. On the door of her refrigerator she left herself notes from those pads where you peel the little yellow sheets off and stick them to things. One of her notes read: AUNT LEAH IN CO above an address in Boulder and a phone number. Another note read: CHUCK BACK MONDAY.

The pad itself sat on top of the fridge with a ballpoint pen beside it. I carried both of these back to her vanity and wrote down the names and phone numbers from the business cards in her makeup drawer. Two of these men had the first name Charles—one named McElroy from a computer firm in New Mexico, the other named Melancon from a company in New Orleans called Lehrer-Farragut. But I wrote down every name, seven of them. It required two sheets from the tiny pad. Then I closed the drawer again and put the pad and pen back where I'd found them.

Somebody walked by outside on the porch, and this person stopped in front of Tara's door. I froze in the kitchenette.

At my side several steak knives stood tall among the pile of silverware in the dish rack. I looked for the thin slit of light at the bottom of the door, but couldn't see it. Night had fallen outside.

Then whoever it was walked off, down the staircase to the yard. A car door opened and closed, and the car drove away.

Hanging from a nail in the wall above the dish rack was a set of keys. I picked them up. I could tell right away that these keys were copies because of their generic bows—the bow is the top part of the key, the part your fingers actually touch when you use it. Only one of the keys wasn't shiny new; it was also the longest of the set. It had a round bow with the letters USPS stamped into it, and the other side said DO NOT DUPLICATE.

# 15

MY TRIP HOME TOOK A LONG TIME, BUT I DIDN'T MIND. I had not seen New Orleans at night except for when I'd first driven in, and that first night I'd been nervous about getting caught before I could drop the car off. The city is actually quite pretty, although the streetcars and the buses don't go up any hills so you can't see very far unless you drive on the Interstate, which is elevated.

The streetcar left me at Canal. A few blocks away I waited for the Esplanade bus at Rampart Street. Two other bus routes use that same stop, and they come much more frequently than the Esplanade. A lot more people ride them, too. This bus stop is right in front of a fast-food chicken restaurant. An older man asked me for money so he could eat and I gave him a dollar, but he didn't go inside the restaurant. That was the last time I ever gave a beggar money.

The bus finally came. We rode down Basin Street a few blocks before looping back to Rampart near an old church, and finally we turned left onto Esplanade. Due either to its many trees or its few streetlamps, Esplanade Avenue was poorly lit at night, except when we crossed under the Interstate and when we reached Broad.

I got off the bus at Broad, carrying Tara's "Anisette" pictures in the plastic bag. The driver's watch said it was a little past ten.

First I went into the all-night doughnut shop on that corner. Three cops in uniform sat at the counter, drinking coffee. The girl behind the counter joked with them about someone they all knew, probably one of her co-workers.

"What you need, baby?" she asked me.

The doughnuts sat in racks behind her, with a selection of special ones displayed in a glass case built into the counter beneath the register.

"What's a 'shoe sloe'?" I asked, pointing at a cardboard sign in the case.

"It's like a king cake," she said, "but shaped like the bottom of your shoe. It's supposed to say 'sole.'"

"Oh." I had never heard of a king cake. They had another thing called a honeymoon, which looked like a regular doughnut lying on its side, covered in icing, with cream filling in the hole. They also had eclairs. "I'll have a chocolate eclair," I decided.

One of the cops asked me, "Where you from?"

"I beg your pardon?" I said.

"You ain't from down here," the cop said. He was a tall black man with his hair permed. "You grow up on the Eastern Seaboard somewheres?"

"Yeah," I said, and grinned. "Baltimore."

"Oh, yeah?" He nodded, proud that he'd pegged me. "You talk like it. I been there once, years ago. It's pretty."

"Not as pretty as New Orleans," I told him.

"No place as pretty as New Orleans," one of the other two cops said.

The girl handed me my eclair in a white paper sack and I left. The cop who'd visited Baltimore wished me a good night.

Out on the sidewalk I ate as I walked to the hardware store. They'd closed at least an hour and a half ago, yet as I came up to the front windows I took care to peer in through the iron gate. No one was inside.

On the ring of copies Pierre had helped me cut the night before, I had both keys for the locks that held the gate down over the front, but entering that way made no sense. Anyone driving past would notice me sliding this giant security gate up to open the front of the building.

Instead I went around through the parking lot to the back door. For a moment I stood there with the key in my hand, checking for witnesses, which is not how I usually behave in that kind of situation. Checking for witnesses alerts anyone who happens to be watching that you're up to something. No one could see me, though. Next door was a soul-food restaurant that the health department had closed months ago, according to Edith, and across the street was a bank. No car passing on Broad traveled slowly enough to even notice me at the back of the parking lot.

I unlocked the door and pulled it open. The alarm beeped. Immediately I punched in the code to make it stop. The door swung shut behind me, making everything pitch-black except the keypad for the alarm. I felt around in the dark and switched on the overhead light in the stockroom.

Now I started to consider my position, in a gingerly way: The overhead lights were too bright. Even with just the stockroom lit, someone outside might glimpse them. One of those three cops could leave that doughnut shop at any time, headed this way, and just the quick burst of light that would escape into the showroom when I opened the door to slip through might catch his eye.

So I got the flashlight Pierre kept on top of the fusebox and I flicked the wall switch off again. Places you know well gain an eerie focus when you first see them by flashlight, yet something else about the stockroom made it even creepier. Exactly what it was, I couldn't say. The shelves held dead still, waiting to pounce.

When I went inside the store itself I cupped my hand over the lens of the flashlight, to mute the beam. I set it lens-down on the counter beside the register. This flashlight had a yellow plastic ring that fastened the bulb chamber to the part with the batteries, and this yellow ring lit up just enough to let me see what I was doing.

I laid the plastic bag with Tara's photos in it on the floor and turned on the key cutter. Nothing happened, so I flicked the switch back and forth a few times. Still nothing. It used one of those detachable plug cords, and I pushed the cord into the socket on the back of the machine to make certain it was connected. For just a second I lifted the flashlight to let me check whether the cutter was plugged in. It was. Pierre had it hooked up through a surge protector, which it shared with some other appliances.

I knelt and pressed the button on the power strip. At once the cutter and the register both came to life. The register printed a receipt.

Headlights from outside ran across the ceiling.

I stood up. I thought somebody had just parked out front. I didn't see anyone, though. I went up to the windows and looked out. The gate was harder to see through from inside because I was farther away from it. Nobody had pulled up, however. Normal traffic passed.

I decided someone must have thrown a U-turn. I hadn't driven since the day I'd arrived, but one thing I'd noticed about New Orleans is that whoever laid out the city plan didn't believe in left turns. Instead you have to make a U-turn half a block later, then return the opposite way to your intersection and make a right. Every street wide enough to have a median works that way.

Back at the counter, I tore the receipt from the register. I had worked alongside this machine for hours at a clip, but only now with it breaking the silence did I notice how loud the thing hummed. Again I picked up the flashlight, and cupped my palm over the lens, then held it up to the board where Pierre hung the blank keys.

When copying keys, you have to match the existing key with a blank one, and if you don't have exactly the right shape on hand, you have to improvise. Naturally the store had no blanks that would easily match a key the US Postal Service specifically wants no one to copy. Rather than the bow, I needed to find the closest match for the key's stem. I held Tara's key against one that matched its width and another that matched its length, and debated which one I should try. After a minute I remembered that I wasn't paying for these things, so I took down one of each.

Something made a noise in the stockroom.

With my foot I turned off the power strip. The register's hum died.

Everything in the building lay perfectly still. I listened.

Just when I had all but told myself I'd imagined it, I heard someone's shoes scrape on the stockroom's cement floor. My neck tingled. Then I heard a voice, low, trying not to be heard. A male voice. The closed door muffled it just so that I couldn't understand what he said.

I turned off the flashlight.

Light shone through the thin slit at the bottom of the door, which meant someone had switched on the overhead fluorescents in there.

My thinking was clear at this point. I reasoned that people burglar-izing a closed hardware store probably wouldn't bring guns. Still, if I heard a voice, that meant there were at least two of them.

I reached down onto the shelf beneath the register. After groping around for a second my hand closed around a heavy wooden handle. I picked the object up: a ballpeen hammer some customer must have returned or decided not to buy.

They'd turned the light on in the stockroom, so I doubted they had flashlights. Probably they would stick to robbing stuff from the stock-room. But they might want cash. They might even be stupid enough to turn the store lights on when they came in here to the register. When they did, they would have me outnumbered. Had there been only one of them, I could have hidden behind the counter, but there were at least two. If they did have guns, the second one would shoot me as soon as I took out the first.

So the best place to wait for them was by the stockroom door. When they opened it, they would reach in first to find the wall switch.

As quietly as possible I crossed the floor, lifting my feet so my boots didn't make any shuffling noise on the tile.

I waited at that door, and waited. Any talking inside the stockroom was low and sparse. I expected to hear them stacking merchandise by the exit, ready to load it outside. They were too quiet in there.

Suddenly the door opened. A man stepped through it.

I sank the hammer into his skull. With one blow I dropped him to the floor. By the time I completed my swing, I already saw that this man was Pierre.

Standing behind him in the stockroom was a girl, very young, her eyes now wide with shock. Time stretched, the way it always does during murder. For one slow heartbeat I tried to think why this girl looked familiar, and I wondered whether Pierre had brought her around the store.

Then she broke for the door to the parking lot. The time she spent turning the knob delayed her enough that I grabbed her by her hair when she was barely a full step out the door. She screamed as I hauled her back inside. Immediately she thrashed her way free of my grip and charged away from me, into the store.

I stared at my empty hands, wondering where I'd thrown the hammer. A dark pool had spread on the floor around Pierre's head.

Inside, the girl had reached the front doors. She was beating on them, howling for someone to come save her.

Despite how hard I work to keep from getting angry, I have sometimes lost my temper with people. It happens. I could never pretend I don't know how that feels. But this was the worst ever, because it wasn't just some flash of rage that someone else provoked. This time I knew full well what I had to march into that room and do.

I don't know a great deal about boots. In the places where I've spent most of my life, wearing even tennis shoes is a hard-won freedom. They want us in slippers as much as possible. If not for the smell and the fungal infections, they would keep us barefoot.

The workboots I had bought just before driving to New Orleans were made in England by a company called Doctor Marten's. They come in different colors, and the black pair I bought have a steel shield over the toe to protect your foot in case it collides with a brick or, say, a nail sticking out from a board.

When I finished stomping the girl's skull in, I tried to hold still and couldn't. I was gasping, evidently because I had been shouting the whole time, trying to drown her screams. I do dumb things like that when I get upset.

To steady my breathing I braced myself against the counter. She lay at my feet. I thought that when I first threw her down she tried to crawl away, but it had all become a blur. Maybe I'd kicked her across the floor. She didn't weigh much.

The door to the stockroom still hung open, with Pierre lying where I'd dropped him. The light from in there made the store around me so visible I could tell even at this distance that the stuff gushing out of Pierre's head wasn't all blood. Anyone outside on the sidewalk could have seen at a glance that there were two bodies sprawled on the floor.

But before I could do anything about that, I needed to stop shaking. I inhaled, held the air in my lungs, exhaled, over and over. Finally a cold sweat broke out on my back and I regained my motor control. My limbs would still tremble once I let go of the counter, I knew.

The light from the stockroom reflected off the photographs of Edith's nieces taped on the wall behind the register. My eyes locked on the one of the three girls standing together. The girl in the middle now lay dead at my feet.

I glanced down. There was not enough left of Jennifer's face now to recognize. Her palate had ripped in half, and her braces still clung to the right side of her upper jaw. The other half of the steel wire had torn free of its moorings and now stuck up into the air like an inch-high antenna. A chunk of pink tooth dangled from its tip.

# 16

THE DOGS MET ME AT MY FRONT DOOR. One of them had shat in the kitchen again, but I didn't stop to clean the floor yet. I took the sewing scissors from on top of my fridge into the bathroom and cut my hair to just above my collar.

No one had oiled these scissors in a long, long time. My hair kept jamming the blades. Short splinters of it slipped down inside the back of my shirt. The bigger tufts landed in the sink or on the floor. I scooped up all the hair and flushed it down the toilet. Then I checked myself in the mirror: My hair looked bad, but it definitely changed my appearance.

In my medicine cabinet was a plastic bottle of peroxide that the previous tenant must have left there. I thought about dyeing my hair blond with it, but I didn't know how much to use or how long to leave it on.

The smell of the dog shit inside started to get to me, so I went in and cleaned the kitchen floor. Stupid watched me, eager to help. After I finished, the kitchen still stank, so I opened the back door to let in some fresh air. Both dogs followed me out to the yard.

Although at least one of them hadn't mastered control of his bowels yet, eating regular meals with a roof over their heads had revived both dogs' spirits. Stupid dashed all around the yard, and now Useless chased him. They paid me almost no mind, except to dart close by my legs every few laps.

I crossed the yard and knocked on Christine's window. She opened it and said, "Hey, sweetie."

"How are you?"

"Just peachy," she said, in a very good mood. "Did you just get home?"

I nodded, studying her eyes. Something wasn't right.

"You feel like coming in and fucking me?" she said. Then she sucked air through her nose, to clear her sinuses.

"Okay," I told her. "Sure. Just let me finish walking the dogs, here."

"Whatever," she said. "How was work?"

"Terrific."

She should have known it was hours later than I would have gotten off work at the store. I didn't point that out to her, obviously, since just then her mistake worked in my favor, but I knew she was high.

"What the hell happened to your hair?" she asked me. Because I was standing in the dark she hadn't noticed right away, even though I looked radically different.

"I got a haircut," I said.

"Oh," she said.

We chatted a little more, then I brought the dogs back to my house. Inside, I went right to my refrigerator and opened the freezer. The package of cocaine I'd taken off Wayne's body lay untouched, still in the plastic bags he had used to store it at Christine's. As I checked on it the thought struck me that I should hide the bag inside an empty box, like an ice cream carton, in case Christine did happen to rifle through my refrigerator.

But she hadn't found it, which meant she'd scored coke from a dealer. I'd believed I had her under control, but it was all a game to her. A game.

Stupid was sniffing a small brown blotch on the kitchen floor. At first glance I assumed I had missed a spot of shit when I'd cleaned up. But no, he licked it.

It was blood, from one of my boots.

Despite coming the whole way home, scraping my feet on the asphalt and sidewalks, I'd carried enough blood into the house to leave a print from the toe of my boot.

"No!" I told Stupid, and pushed him away from the stain. He backed away and watched as I wiped it up with a paper napkin, which I then threw into the trash. I went into the bathroom and wiped down my boots with wet toilet paper. Blood had dried all over the right one.

Afterward I washed my hands and my face, and I said good-bye to the dogs as I headed for the back door. They seemed disappointed that I would leave again so soon after coming home.

"I'll take you guys for a big walk tomorrow," I promised them.

Then I said it again, the way dog owners always do, explaining it carefully: "I'll take you out tomorrow, okay? We'll go for a big walk. All over the place."

They watched, mute. As I opened the door I glanced at the hook on the wall where I kept their leashes, and saw that Stupid's was missing.

I had left it lying on the carpet inside Tara's apartment.

The tiny splinters that had dropped inside my collar when I cut my hair suddenly started digging into my neck. For the fourth or fifth time that night, my blood made a whooshing noise in my ears.

I had left the leash on Tara's floor.

The dogs both tilted their heads, trying to decipher what was bothering me now. My eyes met theirs while I silently sorted through my options. I could go to Tara's and retrieve the leash; she probably would not return home for hours yet. I could just take a cab over and back, too.

But that meant a big risk that a neighbor might spot me. People pay more attention at night, especially in a neighborhood like hers. I'd already gotten the key without any trouble. There was also the smaller risk that she might arrive home to see me coming or going, and she might well recognize me from that morning when Ennis had introduced us. He must have told her about how I got taken out of high school, which would make me stand out in her mind.

Most of all, I just didn't feel like going back out. I wanted to spend the night with Christine. When you have someone you have sex with all the time, the idea of relaxing with her is just more appealing than running around breaking into houses.

"All right, guys," I said to the dogs, and left.

When I arrived at Christine's, she was waiting for me in her bedroom wearing a silk robe with nothing underneath it.

"Christ, that's a bad haircut," she told me. "Turn around."

I rotated, so she could see the back of my head.

"Oh, my God," she said. "You paid someone for that?"

I nodded.

"Who?"

"This barber I found," I said. "I kind of got into a fight with the guy, and he didn't finish it."

She snickered. "It looks like he found out you fucked his sister, or something. Do you want me to fix it?"

She owned real haircutting scissors, and one of those big plastic aprons you wear at a barber's shop. While she got them she had me bring a chair into her kitchen. I sat down and she went to work behind me. When she got around to the front part, I peeked up at her and saw a spot of white powder smeared on the edge of her nose.

Maybe the drug made her focus on cutting hair. Supposedly it intensifies any activity the user finds enjoyable, so that's possible. She spent a long time trimming both sides, making sure they were even. I told her I trusted her judgment, so she stopped asking my opinion.

While I sat there, my mind drifted back to the leash on Tara's floor. When she found an object in her house that she knew didn't belong there, what would she do? Ennis would probably be the furthest thing from her mind, but if she did check on him, she'd see he hadn't been in Louisiana. It seemed to me a lot more likely that she would suspect her landlord or the superintendent, or maybe a handyman doing work around the building. She might not notice the leash for a day or two, and she might not think anything odd about. it. Her apartment was a little too neat for her to not notice the thing at all, but she could easily assume a friend left it, if she ever entertained visitors.

Most important, I didn't think finding a dog leash would send her to her kitchenette to count all her spare keys. She had no other reason to believe an intruder had entered the place, because I hadn't touched anything but the key. And the photos.

The photos.

I sat up, rigid.

"What's the matter?" Christine asked.

"Nothing," I said.

"You look concerned."

I swallowed. "I just remembered," I said, "that it's someone's birthday. I forgot. To send them a card."

"Well, you can send them a belated card," she said. "Those ones are funnier, anyway."

I nodded. Christine stood back to admire her handiwork. My haircut was done.

I'd left the photos of Tara on the floor beside the counter in the store. Next to the power strip. A few feet from Jennifer's body.

# 17

I COULD HAVE GONE BACK TO THE STORE THAT NIGHT. In fact, the idea kept me awake. But retrieving the pictures just wasn't worth the risk. As it was, the cops would probably find them, and maybe a detective would track Tara down to ask if she knew how five nude photographs she had signed wound up in a plastic grocery bag at this crime scene, and she would tell them she had no idea.

Christine discovered I was lying awake beside her, so we did it some more. Then I slept fine. For a few hours, anyway; a dream woke me soon after sunrise, and I didn't think I could go back to sleep, so I left Christine in bed and went to my apartment.

When I originally drove to New Orleans I was on the road during the day a lot, so I'd had to buy sunglasses. I still had them. I also owned a couple of white T-shirts that I wore as undershirts. Because all anyone had seen me wear in New Orleans were workshirts, I figured no one would recognize me dressed in anything else, especially with my hair short.

To complete my disguise, at my bathroom sink I slicked my hair back with water. Then I took some money and Tara's mailbox key and headed out the door.

The Esplanade bus would have taken me where I needed to go, more or less, but I deliberately walked to the bus stop on Broad directly facing the store. Pierre's car still sat in the parking lot. No one had raised the security gate over the front yet.

The bus stop was in front of that bank, which occupied a big plot of property because it had four drive-through tellers. So the bank had a low brick wall right there by the sidewalk, and half a dozen black kids on their way to school sat on this wall waiting for the bus. The kids' school uniform was a yellow shirt and black pants.

"Which bus stops here?" I asked them. They all looked about twelve.

"Broad bus," one kid replied.

"There's only one?"

He nodded. The rest of them stared at me.

I asked him, "Would you know how to get to the post office?"

"Which post office?" he asked. "On Loyola?"

"No, the one on..." I tried to think of the name of this tiny street Ennis said it was on. I gave up. "It's between Saint Charles and Camp."

"All right, you get a transfer," the kid said. "Costs a dime. Then you get off at Canal Street, and take that to Saint Charles. Then you get the streetcar."

I thanked him, and I took a seat on the wall, a little way off from them. Soon a bus came. I stayed on the wall.

"Hey, this is the bus," another one of the kids told me.

"That's all right, thanks," I said. "I'm waiting for my girlfriend first."

The kid shrugged and boarded the bus with his friends. It left. I sat watching across the street.

Another bus came ten minutes later. I let it pass.

Sometime after that a black and white cab pulled to the curb in front of the hardware store. I turned my head slightly toward the direction from which the buses arrived, so if whoever got out happened to look my way it wouldn't seem that I was spying.

It was Edith. She slammed the door and walked around the building to the parking lot. At her first sight of Pierre's car she paused. Then she continued to the building's back door and grabbed the handle, expecting to find it unlocked. It didn't open 'so she knocked. No one answered. Finally she brought her keys out of her purse and unlocked it herself.

When she went inside the building, I wondered why Edith had taken a cab to work. She had her own car, after all. Maybe something had gone wrong with it, or maybe she just didn't feel strong enough to drive since she'd probably been awake all night, wondering where her husband was.

She didn't stay inside the store long.

The click of the bolt as the back door opened reached my ears all the way across Broad. Edith took flight directly toward me, saying nothing, her mad stare locked forward. In that instant she recognized me and knew I had left what she'd found. Her eyes burned into me. All the street noise vanished. I could hear the wind sailing her across the parking lot at me.

A man walking past the soul-food place intersected her path just as she crossed the sidewalk. He did not acknowledge Edith's presence, nor she his, and it struck me that what I saw approaching was not Edith at all but her spirit. Edith's heart could well have stopped at the sight of her husband dead, especially if she somehow guessed the identity of his mistress lying mangled fifteen feet away.

Edith glided into the street without slowing. A panel truck hit her. His brakes screeched, and the car behind him slammed into his rear.

She landed in the gutter and didn't move. The cops arrived right away. A third bus came. I got on it.

I arrived at the post office half an hour before it opened. That gave me some time to sit on a bench in the park across the street while I waited.

This was only the second time I saw morning along Saint Charles Avenue, but already the distinct sweetness of it became plain to me. New Orleans smells nice at dawn and spends the rest of daylight in swift decay. Night renourishes whichever trees and flowers give the sunrise that scent. At eight-thirty in the morning people on the streets trudging to their jobs still hadn't shaken off sleep all the way; the people they became at night would take root later and grow as the day burned on.

Three homeless men sipping beer at another bench ten yards away eyed me critically, probably thinking they might beg me for change. Pigeons strutted past me on the footpath.

As I sat there I came to see Edith's death as a merciful one. It happened in an instant, and she either hadn't expected it or hadn't cared.

Whatever she learned inside the store (in all likelihood, just that someone had killed Pierre) altered her permanently. If I know anything about life, I know how it can change forever in a blink, because of an event you can't control. And again, even if she did see the corpse beside the cash register, she almost surely couldn't have deduced whose body that corpse had been. Having the police tell her that her slut niece had been preying upon Uncle Pierre's urges would have crushed the poor woman.

No, death had taken her, swift and kind. I resolved not to meditate on it any further.

Across the street in the post office, a guard came to the glass front doors and unlocked them. I rose from the bench and went inside.

At one time this post office must have been busier, because a huge lobby sat unused just inside. To the right a door led to a small room with an actual counter and clerks. Ennis's letter had said the mailboxes were to the left. I walked down a long hallway, and at the far end I realized I had traveled up the staff of a giant letter F: Two small dead-end passages ran perpendicular to the hallway, two three-walled rooms lined with mailboxes.

Tara's box was in the second room. As I turned the corner I saw a TV camera mounted in the corner of the ceiling, trained on the mailboxes. Ennis hadn't mentioned that. (These cameras popped up everywhere in the years after I left school, and everyone out in the real world got used to them. When I first went away, they didn't even have cash machines at banks yet.) I had to avoid any gesture that showed I didn't know exactly where I needed to go.

Evidently she had not checked her mail in a few days. I hauled the entire wad out and picked through it. Only her phone bill and the one hand-addressed personal letter in the stack would interest Ennis, I decided, and put the rest back in the box.

The post office was close enough to Canal that I didn't wait for the streetcar to take me back. I walked all the way to that chicken place and waited for the Esplanade bus. By now it was well after nine o'clock, so the students and commuters had finished their rush hour. Only three passengers rode with me, and we all sat many seats apart. I had the entire rear of the bus to myself.

Even fallen to seed, as it was that day, Esplanade Avenue possessed an air of unmatched elegance. I found it much more impressive than Saint Charles Avenue (although I had only traveled as far up Saint Charles as Felicity). Almost all the businesses on Esplanade were vacant, at least from Broad to the Quarter, but people still lived there.

I got off at Broad, headed toward Gentilly. After just a few steps I noticed a huge mob filling the sidewalk a block in front of me. Right away I saw two TV crews.

They had all gathered outside the hardware store.

Something inside me that I keep wound tight began to unravel. Events from the past twenty-four hours flashed in my mind, unbidden. Some things I could not recall immediately after killing Pierre now suddenly shone clear. For one thing, the girl had died from my very first kick.

This fugue that held me there probably only lasted a few seconds. When it ended the scene before me had changed: The TV crews had swung into action. The coroner's men came carrying body bags out of the store, and a man in a suit was giving a statement to the press.

That man was the homicide detective who had come to visit Christine. His eyes met mine across the mob, or they seemed to. Immediately I looked away and started crossing the street. An alarm rang in my head, saying too late, the man saw me and remembers me and he's going to come looking.

I kept walking. I could feel his gaze on my back.

When I got about a block and a half away, I glanced back. The cop in the suit had stopped watching me. Then I remembered that I'd cut my hair and everything. He didn't know me. I was just some face in the crowd, in dark glasses, no less, watching him perform for the TV cameras.

# 18

I ENTERED CHRISTINE'S THROUGH HER KITCHEN DOOR and found her still asleep. On the upper shelf in her closet sat an iron. Quietly I took it and stole back to my house.

In my kitchen I filled the iron and plugged it in. It took a while for the steam to build inside it, so I killed a few minutes playing with Stupid, snapping my fingers above his head to make him lunge at my hand. Now that he'd regained his vigor, the shape of his face betrayed more than ever that one of his parents must have been a full-blood pit bull. He had that square grin. When his lips pulled back from his teeth, his snout looked like a meat-eating dinosaur's.

Steam vapor began to trickle out the top of the iron. I laid Tara's phone bill and letter face-down on the counter, then spread a clean towel from my linen closet on top of them. After one slow pass of the hot iron across the towel, both envelopes peeled open easily. I had to blot the wet glue with the towel so it wouldn't stain the paper.

The itemized page in her phone bill showed collect phone calls from Taipei, a city in Taiwan. That didn't make sense. A gold digger doesn't pay the charges when a mark calls from overseas.

The letter was from Chuck. The postmark said Metairie, Louisiana, which is near New Orleans. Maybe this wasn't the same Chuck she expected home either the day before yesterday or next Monday, according to the memo on her refrigerator.

He wrote the letter by hand on a single sheet of plain white typing paper. He had trouble writing in straight lines, and he'd misspelled several words and used "must of" instead of "must have" in two different places. This didn't seem to me the work of a man who travels internationally for business.

The letter proclaimed his love for her, and told her that he and she needed to keep the faith now especially, when outside conditions meant they had to share their love in secret. In his closing paragraph he mentioned someone named Anna. *It would devastate her and that wouldn't be fair,* he said. *She has never done anything to hurt us and I wish her the best. It's also important to stay friendly in light of the court proceedings ahead.*

Another item that you didn't find everywhere before I went away was the copy machine. Other than in libraries, I don't recall ever seeing one. They didn't work as well as the ones today, either. Back then they used shiny paper that smudged very easily.

But now even the post office had copy machines, so copying Tara's mail would be a convenient way to make Ennis happy. They didn't have a fax machine there, though. Fax machines are the enemy of the post office. If everyone owned a fax machine, we wouldn't need to mail each other anything.

I dumped the water out of Christine's iron as I crossed the lawn back to her house. Again I came in the back door without waking her. I slipped the iron into its spot on her closet shelf and grabbed her extra copy of the Yellow Pages, which I took back to my house.

A store a few blocks up Saint Charles from the post office offered copiers *and* fax service. I memorized the address.

The dogs stared at me dolefully as I prepared to leave the house again. "Guys," I told them, "big walk later. When I get home, okay?" Even Useless acted disappointed. Stupid frowned.

This time I caught the Esplanade bus at the stop closer to my house. When we crossed Broad I saw that most of the crowd had left the crime scene at the hardware store. By the time I returned from this errand, it would all have ended.

Riding the bus so much didn't bother me, so long as I didn't have to ride with lots of other passengers every time. The scenery along the route hadn't become familiar yet. Some of the houses had signs out front declaring them landmarks. On Rampart Street we stopped in front of a church that soldiers had built as a chapel for victims of yellow fever.

At Canal Street, on my way toward Saint Charles, I stopped by a drug store and bought clear nail polish. Then I went to the streetcar stop. It was too crowded. The streetcar looks very old-fashioned, so people who come to New Orleans for vacation want to ride around in it.

It was a nice enough morning, so I walked. I just followed the streetcar tracks up Saint Charles. The air smelled dirtier than it had an hour and a half earlier, for the day had begun to wilt. I reached the copy shop in about fifteen minutes.

A lot of customers milled around in this shop, either using self-serve copiers or waiting to pick up orders they'd placed. The store also rented computer time, so another group of people waited in line to sit at terminals.

After a few minutes I got to use a copier, but it turned out they didn't take money. I had to put a dollar into a separate machine across the room, and this machine spat out a small plastic card with a magnetic strip on the back. All the copy machines accepted these little cards.

So I waited in another line for another copier. This time I copied the front page of Tara's phone bill, the page listing her itemized calls, and Chuck's letter to her.

At various places around the store they had work stations, with pens and markers and glue for customers to use. Standing at one of these tables I carefully folded Tara's mail back into the envelopes and pasted them closed with the clear nail polish I'd just bought. When she opened them, the flap of the envelope would feel completely natural. Had I resealed them with, say, the lipstick-shaped tube of glue supplied by the copy shop, the flap would separate too easily. White liquid glue from a squeeze bottle, on the other hand, would fasten it too well, and probably leave suspicious wrinkles in the paper when it finally dried.

When I finished, I noticed some woman with brown hair watching me. I almost expected her to say something, but instead she shrugged to herself and resumed stapling together sets of copies.

After that I stood in line to get to the front desk. You couldn't use the fax machine yourself; you had to fill out a cover sheet and let the clerks actually send it. So I waited there, not paying much attention, until I glanced over my shoulder and caught the brown-haired woman studying me again. When I turned around to meet her gaze, she pretended to immerse herself in her paperwork.

Now I deliberately avoided turning around. I had six people ahead of me in the line. Seconds crawled past, became a minute. The line did not move.

Someone appeared next to me, and I flinched.

It was that same brown-haired woman. She pretended to survey a rack of office supplies, like scotch tape and staples and so on.

The envelopes. She was trying to peek at the address on the envelopes in my hand.

When she'd seen me reseal the phone bill, she'd realized what I was doing, that I must be returning it to someone's mailbox somewhere, and if she could see the victim's address, she could send a warning there: *Someone's spying on you.* Never mind that it wasn't my idea in the first place, or that I didn't have any choice but to do what Ennis wanted.

I bolted off the line and out of the store.

Rather than return right to Saint Charles, I walked the cross street in the opposite direction, and made the first turn I could, down a dingy street only one block long. No doors faced the sidewalk on either side of this street, which was really more a paved alley between two block-sized sets of commercial buildings. This street probably only existed for the purpose of deliveries.

Halfway down the block I waited to see if the woman tried to tail me. She didn't show.

I took the Camp Street way back to the post office. Three minutes later as I left to return home, I marveled at this nosy woman's gall. Her amateur-detective act had so unnerved me that I'd heedlessly replaced both envelopes among Tara's untouched mail, right in full view of the TV camera. I needed to be more subtle. If some postal worker on coffee break happened to look at the monitor at that moment, he or she might ask why I was putting mail into a box and not taking any away.

# 19

INSTEAD OF GETTING OFF AT BROAD, I RODE the bus up Esplanade to a pet store, where I bought Stupid a new leash—a plastic handle with a sixteen-foot cord spooled inside it. A thumb switch locked the cord at any length I wanted. It looked like a toy block-and-tackle.

This time when I came home Christine had woken up. She was in her kitchen, frying two eggs. "Where did you go?" she asked me.

"I went downtown," I said, "to see about a job."

"Don't you work at a hardware place?"

"Yeah, I was doing that, but I quit," I told her. "Not enough money."

"You only been there a week," she said. "Where's this job you went to look at?"

"Oh, a store," I said. "They make copies and things."

"You ever work in a copy shop before?"

I shook my head. "Thought it might be interesting."

"I need a job myself," she announced as she placed both eggs and a slice of toast on a plate and handed it to me. "I was thinking about going down the Quarter this afternoon, actually."

I thanked her and ate. While I did, I decided I'd made the right choice by not faxing Ennis yet. I'd do better to wait another day or so, until I could tell him more. If I could definitely tell him the name of the man who had stolen Tara, plus a little bit about their affair, that might satisfy Ennis right there, and I wouldn't have to spy anymore for him.

The afternoon was warm. I painted the driveway gate that ran between Christine's house and the bar. I took my time. The dogs chased each other around the yard while I worked. A little after two, Christine called herself a cab and left. As soon as the car pulled away I went into her house through the back.

I sat down with her phone in the bedroom. From my pocket I dug out the yellow memo on which I had written the two phone numbers of men named Charles from Tara's makeup drawer. I called the local one, Melancon.

A receptionist answered by saying, "Lehrer-Farragut," the name of the company. She should have wished me a good afternoon after that, or asked how she could help me. People aren't very professional in the South.

"Say, I'm a friend of Chuck Melancon's," I introduced myself, and paused.

"Yes, sir?" she greeted me, which told me that, yes, callers normally referred to this man as Chuck.

"And I just wanted his address, real quick," I said.

"Sir, I can't give that information over the phone," she said.

"No, I mean the address there," I told her, "at the office. I need to send him something."

"Do you want to speak to him?"

"No," I said. "It's a surprise. I'm mailing him an invitation to my wedding."

"Oh, okay," she said, relieved, and then she gave me their address. I pretended to write it down.

When she finished, I said, "He's back in town now, isn't he?"

"Chuck? Yes, he came back on Monday."

"Where was he this time, China?"

She wanted to get to another call, I could tell. "No, that was two weeks ago, Taiwan. This time he was just in California."

I thanked her and hung up.

It surprised me to find so many Melancons in the phone book. I'd never before heard of anyone's having that name. There were three named Charles, two with just the initial C, and a single Chuck, at an address in a place called Lakeview.

So I called Chuck, and a woman answered.

"I'm sorry, this may sound dumb," I said, "but I discovered this phone number in my pocket, and I'm at a loss for who gave it to me. Does a Chuck live at this number?"

"Yes, my husband," the woman said.

"How would I know him?" I asked.

"He works at Lehrer-Farragut," she said.

"What's that?"

"They do contracting for the government," she explained. "Defense contracts. Ships and things."

"Wait, someone told me something like that," I said, straining my memory. "He said he was going to Taiwan."

"Yes! That's Chuck," the woman said.

"But where would I have met him?" I asked.

This woman's friendly, helpful manner had already won me over. She thought for a moment and then said, "Oh, wait. Have you ever eaten at Balconis?"

I asked her to repeat the name.

"Balconis, like balcony only with an -is at the end," she said. "It's a Mediterranean restaurant in the French Quarter. He's there all the time."

"Is it a place on a balcony?" I asked, which was a stupid thing to ask, but I was nervous.

"No," she said, "a little Creole cottage. It's not far from Saint Peter Street on Burgundy. He eats there a lot. It's his sister's restaurant."

"Yeah, that's right," I said. "That guy Chuck. I know who you mean now. You must be Anna, then."

"Yes, I am," she said. "And you're...?"

"Chuck told me about you," I said. "I can't wait to meet you. We should all get together sometime. My wife likes Chuck, she thinks he's funny."

"I look forward to meeting you both," Anna said. "Who should I tell Chuck was calling?"

"My name's Louis," I said.

"Well, all right, Louis, I'll be sure to let him know you called," she told me, cordially informing me by her tone that our conversation would now end. Oh, I liked this woman.

The phone book listed Balconis's number and address. I called and asked about reservations. A college-age girl assured me the whole night was wide open. I asked if I needed a tie and she said no, just a jacket. I said I'd call back in a few minutes.

Rather than hang the phone up in its cradle, I held it in my hand with my thumb pressing the rectangular button to disconnect the line. For some reason I couldn't shake the suspicion that I needed to call someone else. That didn't make much sense, since I didn't know anyone in New Orleans. I certainly couldn't risk calling Ennis from Christine's phone.

Finally I decided to try Balconis again, to squeeze a little more information about Chuck from the hostess. I lifted the phone to my ear and released the button.

Instead of a dial tone, the calm rustle of some kind of business office greeted me. I said, "Hello?"

"Yes, hi, may I speak to Christine Paffgen?"

"Uh, she's not here," I said, suddenly grasping that I'd accidentally answered the phone before it rang.

"This is Detective Earl Holland," the man said. "Who am I speaking to, please?"

"Louis," I told him. "I'm Christine's friend."

"Oh, we met the other day," he said. It was that same cop. No one had told him my name was Louis, by the way. "Can you give Christine a message for me, please?"

"Surely," I said, and wrote down his phone number, though I'm sure he'd given it to her when he'd visited the house. He explained what he needed to ask her, but finding myself on the phone with him flustered me so badly that I only pretended to listen.

He thanked me and we hung up. After hearing his voice I lacked the strength of mind to scam data out of the restaurant, so I put that call off to another time. Instead I sat in Christine's bedroom talking to myself. I do that sometimes, though it's never as obvious to other people as I always think it would be.

My more rational side took over when I had to come up with a reason to give Christine why I was using her phone when she wasn't home. If I didn't give her his number to call, the cop would definitely call back and say he'd left the message with Louis, and Christine didn't know me by that name. I had to tell her.

So I decided to say I'd answered the cop's call by accident while phoning to see about my mythical copy-shop job. An excuse always works better when I base it on a story they heard before I needed them to excuse me, I find. Something a person already "knows" provides a firm foundation.

Once I'd worked that out, my panic from talking to the cop vanished. I realized that his chatting with me now meant he hadn't recognized me this morning outside the hardware store. I still needed to keep out of his way, because if he saw me with my hair cut he just might recall seeing me in the crowd on Broad, but for now he didn't know who I was. It proved to me that I had to avoid getting paranoid.

# 20

IN NEW ORLEANS, THERE ARE LOTS OF RATS and lots of coincidences. Instead of squirrels they have rats climbing trees and scampering from roof to roof along phone lines. The rats aren't afraid to run around in broad daylight, either. Most of them look big enough that they probably don't need to worry much about cats.

One lay flattened by cars on the asphalt of Burgundy Street, with all its blood long since evaporated, its fur somehow still intact. The sun had baked this carcass a dust color with hints of light brown. My sunglasses made the white parts appear blue.

I couldn't see much of Balconis, only the front. First I walked right past it, peering inside the windows and skimming the menu they kept in a glass box mounted on the building's face. The food was fairly expensive. To enter the restaurant you had to walk down a sort of driveway, paved with patio-style slate instead of concrete. At the front of this passage stood a black gate of wrought-iron spokes that formed a half circle with its flat side down. At the other end of the passage another identical gate sealed off a back yard full of plants. A little farther than midway to the back was the door. I watched a young couple enter.

But I couldn't stand there gawking. Down the block where the rat lay crushed I stood next to a mailbox and watched the traffic in and out of Balconis. Maybe a dozen people came out and hailed cabs. Only two cabs dropped people off. Probably the people leaving had just finished a late lunch, and the new arrivals were early for dinner.

A taxi dropped off a third couple, an older man and a young blonde. For a flash I thought I'd seen the girl before. By the time I thought it might be Tara, they had already disappeared down the driveway.

I gave them a few minutes to get seated. Then I began to think of excuses to walk past the restaurant again. I didn't want anyone to notice me hovering around out front. A place like that might pay attention. A good alibi is one you think out before someone asks for it.

For inspiration I looked around at the people passing by on the sidewalk. There weren't very many.

From the other direction came a guy whose face I recognized. That hardly seemed possible, and I almost dismissed the idea and looked away. But my eyes locked on his for a flash, and I knew where I'd met him: outside Cody's bar, during Jazz Festival. His name would not come to me.

He glanced at me and then studied the wall next to him, then glanced back. The sight of me made him nervous, I think. My mind raced, trying to recall his name.

"Gary," I said.

"Yeah?" Right away it relieved him to learn he actually knew me, though he hadn't any idea who I was.

"Hey, how are you doing?" I asked.

He said he was doing fine, on his way to work. He slowed down but didn't stop walking. I fell in alongside him. No one in Balconis would look twice at me if I passed with a friend.

"You remember me?" I said. "From Jazz Festival? You came to the bar where I was working."

"No, I'm afraid I don't," he said.

"Remember? I helped you get a cab?" I racked my brain for anything else he might have told me. "You told me about that guy, that friend of yours, he got so dosed up on acid, he showed up at his mother-in-law's restaurant wearing underwear and a Doctor Seuss hat during—"

Snickering, Gary shushed me, looking around to make sure no one else had heard what I'd just said.

"Yeah, man, I remember you now, you were the doorman," he said. "Don't gab about that, man. That guy's my manager at work."

"Oh, yeah?" I said, making conversation. We were about to reach the gated driveway of Balconis. "Where do you work?"

"Right here," Gary said, and pointed down the alley. "Balconis. You ever see this place?"

I shook my head, so he brought me down the alley to show me. The back yard was a patio, much bigger than I'd expected. People sat eating at glass tables. Everyone had expensive clothes on.

"You cut your hair," he said. "That's why I didn't know you."

"Yeah," I said. "It got hot."

"Ha! You don't even know 'hot.' Wait another month."

The building itself was a one-story cottage, with a separate building in the back that Gary called a slave quarter. As he walked me back down the alley toward the street, I could see inside the main room of the restaurant. Tara was sitting at a table beside a window, with a man in his late fifties. She didn't notice me, but the man did. He thought he'd caught me ogling his girl.

Gary just happened to glance up as we passed, and once we got past the window, he said in a low voice, "Jesus H. Christ. That guy, what a douchebag. You see that guy?"

"Who?" I asked.

"That guy who was staring at us out the window. Real piece of shit. He's here all the time. His sister is the chef, so he brings his fucking mistress here 'cause he's a *cheap* piece of shit. Meanwhile we all know his wife. Everybody in this fucking place is friends with his wife."

"Wow," I said. We had reached the sidewalk again.

"Yeah, that's his table, by the window there." Gary sighed, shaking his head, sad. "One time I had to move a family of paying customers because he shows up and they're sitting at *his* reserved table by the window. Now he brings his little stripper tramp here."

I laughed, since he seemed to want me to. Then Gary said, "I'm sorry, I'm really bad with names. What's your name again?"

"Louis Collins," I said. We shook hands.

"I'll see you around, Lou, take care," Gary said as he walked back down the alley to work.

For some reason I stood there another minute by myself. Having everyone in the place think I was Gary's friend meant no one cared if I lingered in the alley. It seemed very quiet and peaceful. An elderly couple walked past me on their way inside, and they both nodded hello to me.

When I turned to leave, I found a teenager with long hair standing in front of me. He mumbled something.

"What?" I asked.

"Is this Balconis?"

I nodded.

"I'm the guy Father LaSalle sent over," he said. He kept his hands in his pockets. When he saw I did not know what he meant, he said, "From Covenant House."

"What's that?"

"You know, Covenant House?" he said. "It's where I'm staying at."

"I don't know what you mean," I said.

"Covenant House. It's, like, all kids who ran away—well, I didn't run away exactly, but," he explained. He went on to recount how he ended up at this shelter. I listened. At last he said a priest there had sent him here to wash dishes, with the promise of forty dollars and a meal afterward.

Obviously he thought I worked there at the restaurant.

"Sorry I'm late," he said. "I mean, just a few minutes, but."

"That's okay. Go on in to the kitchen," I told him. "Ask the girl at the desk to show you."

I made a right turn onto the sidewalk, and then turned again to get off Burgundy Street. In the window of a bar on the corner a clock said it was a quarter past four. A few blocks. away, toward the river, Bourbon Street had just begun to wake up.

I came back to Burgundy around five o'clock, since they'd only just gotten to the restaurant when I'd left. Chuck would definitely keep her there at least an hour. A guy playing the big shot on the cheap wants his money's worth.

Half a block up the street a private house had a couple of concrete steps at its front door, where I sat down and watched Balconis. A few cabs dropped well-dressed people at the big black gate. Not much else happened on that block. Anyone on foot was headed somewhere else. The bar on the corner stayed so quiet I assumed it was empty until a tall guy dressed as a woman came out. Without even glancing around he left for Rampart Street, the opposite direction from Bourbon.

After half an hour a taxi brought a blonde woman in a green suit. As she entered the gate, a man hollered from somewhere I couldn't see. The cab began to pull out but jerked to a stop. Chuck and Tara emerged from the alley; he opened the cab's back door for her and they kissed. They chatted for a minute more before she climbed in. Chuck watched the cab move away down Burgundy until it turned left onto a sidestreet. Then, shaking his head a little as if recalling something funny, he went back inside his sister's restaurant.

I didn't follow Tara's cab. I didn't need to. Tara had gone to work. Ennis had told me which clubs she danced at.

Chuck stayed in the restaurant for at least another hour. After a very long time I walked past the front of Balconis again, peering in the windows. A young couple sat at the table where I'd seen Chuck earlier. For a moment I worried that he might have left the building through some other exit I didn't know about. Then I glimpsed him deeper back in the restaurant, standing at a bar.

I hadn't noticed this bar back there before, but now the sky had darkened enough that someone had turned up the lights inside the restaurant. Now I could easily see everything inside, all the carved woodwork and the candle sconces on the walls. Unconsciously I must have known that this shift in the lighting meant anyone inside Balconis could see me a little less well, for I stood there studying the place and the people inside. I saw more waitresses than waiters, and the waiters all seemed gay. The staff behaved like a huge family serving a holiday dinner.

I probably stood there longer than I should have, but no one in Balconis noticed. Just when I returned to the steps in front of that house up the block, a cop car passed me. They paid me no mind, but they might notice if they passed again and saw me still sitting there. A light discussion with cops I could handle—authority figures don't particularly make me upset—but I had no way to know how well my Louis Collins papers would hold up if they asked for ID. I didn't have a driver's license, for one thing, or credit cards. In Louisiana they can lock you up for not having ID, because that violates the Napoleonic Code. That's what Pierre told me.

In the Quarter Burgundy Street runs one-way towards Esplanade Avenue, so to watch oncoming traffic and the restaurant at the same time I needed to walk past the windows yet again and take up a position on the other side. Before I made up my mind to do it, though, Chuck walked out of Balconis.

He stumbled a little as he came toward me, maybe because of the ragged state of the sidewalk. I held still with my eyes locked on the ground. Chuck passed not two feet from me and never thought to look at my face.

When he'd almost reached the cross street, I began following him. He continued straight up Burgundy to a parking lot a block before Canal Street, where he got into a tan BMW. When he pulled out, he chose an exit on the far side of the lot, so I never saw his license plate.

After Chuck took off, I went to Bourbon Street again, to find which club Tara was at that night. As I walked there I steeled myself for what the places would be like: Women would traipse around naked, laughing and getting guys to give them money. I just had to act businesslike, and not give anyone the chance to provoke me.

It turned out not to be that bad, actually. The first place I went looked sleazy on purpose, with glowing orange spraypaint on the walls and biker music, but no one in there seemed especially roguish. The clientele were all men in T-shirts they obviously had bought during their visit, because the shirts said things about New Orleans. Most of these guys were in their forties or fifties, I'd say.

After spending just shy of two decades—almost two thirds of my life—under the scrutiny of men trained to police my every move, I found it no challenge to pass unseen among regular people. Being the kind of person to whom regular people would only pay attention if they wanted something also probably helped. No one at this strip club even made me buy my minimum drink.

But these other guys, these older men, milling around the way I remember kids standing at a freshman mixer, too shy to ask any girl to dance but drooling over them anyway—these men could hide nothing about themselves: They would give anything to have young girls naked near them. I couldn't help seeing through this place.

When not onstage the dancers sat at tables in the back of the club, where it was dark. A few customers sat with them back there. One man had a girl straddling his lap, sliding back and forth on him, her eyes closed and her lips pursed. I couldn't understand how come that was legal if prostitution isn't. I didn't see Tara anywhere, so I left.

The next place Ennis had told me about had a sign at the front door calling it a "gentleman's club." They charged ten dollars at the door, and as soon as you got to the room where the stage was, a girl in tights came and made you order a six-dollar drink. Money didn't matter to me, since I still hadn't spent half of what the chop shop paid me for the car I drove down.

The girls looked healthier than the ones at the previous bar. Five of them danced at a time, one on a main stage with a pole and the others on smaller platforms surrounded by armchairs. Any girl not dancing didn't sit around smoking, either, though a sign offered something called a table dance.

The record changed to old-sounding jazz with a banjo and clarinets and everything. A new girl came on the main stage, dressed like a school-child. Her hair reached her waist. She wriggled out of her outfit, making coy faces. The way men leered back at her began to trouble me, but I beat the feeling down. When I looked back up, the girl smiled directly at me.

It was Tara, wearing a wig. Just for that split second I thought she knew who I was. But right away I could see that the stage lights would keep me invisible to her. They use a lot of psychology when they build clubs like that—the clientele prefers to sit in the shadows. These men don't want anyone to see them act that way. I can't blame them.

Once I recognized her, it surprised me that I'd mistaken Tara's wig for real hair even at a glance. Probably a lot of dancers wear cheap wigs to disguise themselves, but this thing really stood out, partly because it hung all the way to her waist but mostly for its ratty condition. I doubt many customers complained, though.

Another waitress in tights appeared beside me and asked, "Can I get you another drink?"

"I'm fine," I said.

"No, you have to buy a drink," she said.

"I already did."

As she spoke she pushed her eyeglasses up the bridge of her nose. This girl wasn't pretty enough to dance here. "That was during last set, sir," she said, by rote. "There's a one-drink minimum per set."

"A set of what?" I asked.

"Each time a new dancer comes on stage, it's a new set."

"Oh," I said, and reached in my pocket. I handed her a ten. "I'll just have a soda."

"Are you sure?" she said. "It's still going to cost you six dollars."

"That's all right," I told her.

The waitress went off to fetch my drink. I turned back to the show. Tara had bared her breasts now, and she paced back and forth across the stage playing with them. Either she knew certain men sat at certain tables, or she could sense which tables in the darkened house she affected most strongly.

The other girl came back with my soda. It was cola with a lime in it. When she tried to hand me my change, I said, "Keep it."

"Oh, thanks," she said, surprised. Probably my trying not to buy a drink had led her to expect I'd stiff her.

"What's your name?" I asked her.

She told me, and I talked to her for a few minutes. Business wasn't too brisk that night, I suppose. Normally I would have avoided talking, but it made me feel superior just then, chatting with this stranger while watching Tara manipulate these weak, gullible men.

After she finished her set, Tara came down and sat at a table with several men who were about Chuck's age. They laughed a lot. The waitress by now knew me well enough that she let me slide for the third drink. I pretended to watch the next dancer, a girl of medium height with straight black hair cut the blunt way Japanese women wear it, actually much better-looking than Tara. I caught myself growing a little angry that a woman so beautiful should sell herself in this vulgar pit.

That told me I needed to get out of there. If I know anything, I know when to quit. I didn't have much to learn from watching Tara, anyway. Mostly I just wanted to see what her life was like.

# 21

WHEN I GOT HOME, I WAS IN THE MOOD to have sex. For once the dogs had not shat in my kitchen while I was out. I fed them and we went out to the yard.

Both dogs had regained their vitality. Having to leave them inside all day bothered me. Right away they both crapped in the yard, almost at the same time, so I praised them both, then I buried it with the shovel from the shed. Useless had already been been housebroken once, I could tell. Stupid followed what Useless did.

Today even Useless wanted to play. They chased each other back and forth. They barely noticed when I opened the back gate to Christine's house.

"Hey?" I called.

After two seconds she said, "Yeah?" Just from that tiny pause I could tell I had surprised her.

"It's me," I told her.

"I know it's you," she said. "What's up?"

I found her sitting on her bed. "Nothing, I just wanted to see how you are," I said.

"Fine," she said. "I'm fine."

She'd hidden the coke on the floor underneath her bed. By her foot I glimpsed a china plate, which at least meant she was snorting lines rather than shooting it.

"What do you feel like doing tonight?" I asked.

"I don't know," she answered, tilting her head, staring at the wall. "I could go out. Do you feel like going out? We could go dance or something."

I didn't answer. A cloud of anxiety I could all but see formed around her as she resisted her need to look in my eyes, to make sure I didn't know about the coke. That's how drugs ruin your life: They make you play tricks on people who know you too well to fall for them.

In silence I studied Christine's neck and what I could see of her face, and she held her gaze upon a small poster hanging next to her closet. Her room was dim and sad. And still I wanted to fuck her. You get used to it, and you start wanting it more. It's like a drug.

Finally I said, "Oh, that cop called for you."

That gave a reason for her to face me. "What cop?"

"The one who was here. I can't think of his name," I said. "He came to talk to you about Wayne."

"Oh. What do you mean, he called for me?" she asked. "He came by the house today?"

"No," I said. "He called up."

"What were you doing answering my phone?" Just like that, the stuff soured her mood. I didn't like her tone of voice.

"I was painting the fence," I told her.

She interrupted me and said, "So you start answering my phone? I need to get messages from people. Don't answer my phone, all right?"

"I didn't."

"Then how come you talked to him?"

"Look, I'm sorry," I said. I just wanted her to stop snapping at me. "It was an accident."

"An accident," she repeated, like a lawyer belittling someone's testimony.

"I came inside—"

"And the phone flew through the air into your hand." She clapped her hands together once and stood up, smirking at me.

"I came inside while I was painting—"

"Or did someone drive a car into my phone and it landed on you?"

"—painting the fence," I went on, my voice growing slightly louder through no choice of mine, "and I came in to drink some water in your kitchen, and I walked in here—"

"Don't answer my phone, okay? That's all."

No arguing with her. Yet I could sense somehow that pointing out the coke beneath her bed would not help my position in the long run. Better she should think I didn't know.

"Did he want me to call him?" she asked, suddenly civil again.

I nodded. Her venom had rattled me enough that I didn't think to fish the cop's number out of my back pocket. Instead she looked him up in her address book. She dialed his beeper number.

When she hung up the phone I came up behind her and put my arms around her. It started happening. All the heat that had risen inside me during her snit now fueled my urge to put it into her. I held her against the wall. She fought back but didn't mean it. Resisting was a game for her. I couldn't have pulled her jeans off if she didn't want me to. Between her legs it was wet before I even touched her there.

I didn't bother kicking off my sneakers or stepping all the way out of my pants. I just slid them down to my knees and put myself inside her from behind. In the short amount of time we'd been together, I'd discovered that I liked doing it to her that way, standing up and backwards. The coke must have made it easy for her to get ready fast, because right away she was grinding so I would jab deep into the parts where she liked it the most. The size of me made her cry out. Her whole body quaked.

The doorbell rang.

Christine pushed me away, and I dropped onto the bed. While I struggled to pull my pants back up, she went into her living room and called out, "Hello?"

"Is Christine Paffgen home?" a man's voice called from out on the front steps.

"Who's there?"

"It's Detective Holland. You beeped me."

"Yeah, I'm here," she said. "Can you wait a second? I was expecting you to call me before you came over."

"I happened to be in the neighborhood. I only need to talk to you a minute," he said.

"That's all right, I just need to put clothes on. Hold on." She came back into the bedroom. Rather than her jeans, she slipped into a pair of shorts. Then she knelt beside the bed and slid the coke plate farther underneath, so it wasn't visible at all in case the cop came in this room. I acted as if I didn't notice what she was moving or why.

When Christine opened the front door, the cop said, "Sorry, didn't mean to catch you at a bad time."

"No, that's all right, come in. I just needed to put clothes on," she assured him.

He entered the living room. From the bedroom doorway I nodded hello to him. He gave me an odd look. Quickly I turned my back and started for Christine's back door. "I need to go walk my dogs," I called out to her. "I'll be back in half an hour or so."

"Okay," she called back.

As I passed through her kitchen it occurred to me that he might remember seeing me in the crowd outside the hardware store that morning. But that thought didn't panic me at all, because the look I'd seen on his face didn't seem to mean he was jogging his memory. No, he'd been trying to decide something about my appearance, and he himself probably didn't know exactly what it was.

One thing I knew for sure: This detective had talked to Freddy from the hardware store about me. Could Freddy describe me well enough for the cop to recognize me? Maybe they had brought in a sketch artist. But I looked different with my hair short.

In any case I wanted to stay clear of this cop. The dogs came to meet me as I stepped out Christine's back door. They walked with me around the house. I'd opened all the shutters that afternoon when Ennis called, so tonight I could see the cop talking to her inside the living room, though I couldn't hear what they said. She was sitting on her couch and he stood in the middle of the room, questioning her but not in an antagonistic way. From her face I guessed she was answering him honestly but found his questions startling. Then again, maybe the coke caused her to overdo her earnestness.

All at once Christine turned toward the window. I thought her eyes had fallen upon me, and I dodged close to the house. But she hadn't seen me. Anyway, I could have just said I was rounding the dogs up. When I crept back into view again, she was handing something small to the cop. I couldn't see what it was.

I led the dogs back to my house. We had to go in through my back door and then out again through the one that opened onto the side alley. Quietly we passed Pat's door. I could hear his television.

We walked up the block to Gentilly. Cody had opened the bar tonight. I'd planned on watching the cop leave Christine's from the corner, but the glow from the beer sign in the window and the slight hum of people inside meant I needed a new plan.

Cody's customers had already taken all the parking spaces at this intersection. As I stood there, trying to decide whether to watch from up the block or from across the street by the entrance to the racetrack, a car parked down by my house. A red-haired guy younger than I was climbed out. To reach the bar he had to pass me. I didn't look him in the eyes.

Just after he passed, he said, "Hey, Whitey."

I glanced up at him and he smiled.

"What?" I asked.

"I said, 'Hey, Whitey.'"

His face didn't look the least bit familiar. "I'm sorry," I said. "Do I know you from work?"

He shook his head, then broke into a smile. "Nope," he told me. "I just saw your nametag."

I was wearing my Whitey shirt. That's why the cop had stared at me in Christine's room: He couldn't recall where he'd heard the name Whitey recently, but in the back of his mind he knew someone had used it. Having no reason to connect Christine to the hardware store had kept him from placing it.

The red-haired guy went in the bar. I spun around to bring the dogs home. This shirt belonged in the garbage, or not even. Burned, better.

Going home so soon after leaving the house always pisses off dogs. They just won't believe that you're only going back for a minute. They mope as if you're ending their summer vacation two weeks early.

So they sulked back to the house with me, down the alley past Pat's door to the back of the house. To placate them I didn't even take them off their leashes. I placed the leashes' handles on the ground and dug my keys out of my hip pocket.

Through the door I could see a light shining inside my bedroom. I hadn't left one on.

Very quietly I unlocked the door, turned the knob, and slid it open.

Stupid charged inside, his leash dragging on the floor behind him. He disappeared into the bedroom. A second later a man hollered in surprise.

Useless followed Stupid. I got there last.

Blood was spraying from the wound where Stupid had bitten a chunk out of the cop's cheek. The cop had one of my sneakers in his right hand. He swung it repeatedly at Stupid's face. Then Useless came at him, barking, and the cop swung at Useless. Instantly Stupid had his jaws locked on the cop's forearm.

"Call them off!" he shrieked at me.

Time stretched a little. Without even wondering about it, I knew the cop had not drawn his gun because he had it in an ankle holster; bending down would have let the dogs at his face again. As he reached down frantically with his free left hand, I knew he couldn't easily get the gun out, since he would of course wear his holster on his right ankle. I even knew why he had my sneaker in his hand: He'd snuck in here trying to find shoes that matched the bloody footprints he'd found in the hardware store.

And of course I knew if he got his gun out, both dogs would die, right now in front of me, and then I would go back where I'd come from. For good.

No fucking way. From the windowsill I grabbed the heavy iron shelf rack, the one I used to prop the window open. I advanced on him and swung it. First I grazed the side of his head. Normally he would have reacted more, but at that moment he had a pit bull clamped on him, so all he did was wince.

I hit him on the shoulder, then the neck. He didn't shout any more orders at me. He didn't even scream for help. Suddenly he tried to lunge for the iron rail in my hand, but too slowly. I brought it down as hard as I could, and smacked it square into his arm, halfway between his elbow and his wrist. Bone cracked.

I brought the rail down again, closer to his hand. The cop grunted, not out of fear but from shock. I thought he'd pulled his hand away. He hadn't. The blow had broken both bones so cleanly that his wrist and hand now hung limp at a right angle from the rest of his arm.

Both of us stared in amazement. It appeared as though his arm now had a second elbow.

I brought the brass rail down on the cop's skull three or four times. He slid down the wall onto the floor, and Stupid went to work on his face. Soon time returned to normal.

# 22

What I did next sounds reckless if you don't understand how the police investigate murders. They don't deal in truth, or justice or whatever. Homicide detectives identify things: a victim, a set of tools, a motive, and whoever did it.

It used to be a lot easier to get away with killing. I don't mean when I was younger, but before World War One. Back then if you didn't leave a witness, or bury someone under your flowerbed, only your own confession would hang you. On the rare occasions that reliably handled evidence was available, juries didn't trust scientists. Fingerprints were all you needed to worry about. Forensics couldn't link a bloodstain to a particular body, or even prove the blood came from a human being.

All that's changed now. Today they'll trace rug fibers tangled in a dead man's beard, or an invisible shred of flesh caught beneath his fingernail. If in his death throes he inhaled a few dog hairs from the floor, they scrape those out of his sinuses and locate the dog by its DNA. They can tell the guy ate a shrimp sandwich six hours before he died. They can tell what state the shrimp came from, whether the dead man liked mayonnaise, what brand of soap he used to wash his hands after he ate.

One thing they can't do is ask the victim where it happened. That's the element you have to play against them nowadays: Keep the cops from finding the crime scene. Without it, they have no way to match their splinters and stains to anything.

So I didn't chop this particular thing into pieces. It wasn't just that I'd lost my nerve after doing Wayne, though that one had gone nasty. Of course Wayne wasn't the first one I ever had to do, but the smells that came out of him shook me up. If I'd ever gutted a deer, I would have known better than to punch a hole in the actual stomach. But you learn. The first time I ever dismembered a body, I didn't know enough to make sure the heart stopped beating first, so the thing wound up spraying the ceiling. That's an easy way to get caught, since the ceiling's hard to clean properly. Cops will look for stains up there, too, if the coroner tells them an artery opened while the victim was alive.

By the time I calmed down, Stupid had retreated from the cop's ruined face. I wasn't sure what kind of noise I'd just made. Sometimes I holler pretty loud when I get upset.

Right away I went outside and padded down the alley to Pat's door. Other than an audience roaring on his television, nothing inside sounded any different. A picture of Pat dozing in his chair formed in my mind. If he'd heard anything from my apartment, it probably wound up as sound effects in whatever he was dreaming. Even if I had roused him, he'd probably blame it on the television and fall back asleep in seconds.

So I went back to my door, glad to have just avoided a possible complication, when all of a sudden the question came to me: How did this cop get inside my apartment?

This time when I went inside I checked the door to the yard. He hadn't closed it all the way, so I swung it open. The key was still in the lock, and a full ring of keys dangled from it. I yanked it out and closed the door.

Christine had given him these keys. They were her master set for all the houses Alva owned. Maybe that's what I saw her hand him when I spied on the two of them. The problem for me now was determining what the cop had told Christine. It didn't seem logical that he would've discussed the hardware store with her. Still, stranger things have happened, particularly in New Orleans.

I entered my bedroom intending to take the cop's pistol so I could bring it to Christine's. Before I even bent down to pull the gun from its holster I changed my mind: If she put herself in a position where something bad had to happen, I couldn't shoot her. Not with the bar next door to her house full of customers. It would have to be my bare hands, and it would have to be quick.

Outside my back door I heard that small grinding thump of bare feet climbing the steps, sliding just barely on the wood because of sand or grit on the soles. The dogs heard it, too; I heard them both rise to greet her. Christine had come to my door, and the cop's logic in leaving the keys in the lock struck me now: He had meant to enter, check my boots or at least find my shoe size, and leave. So he'd left the bolt retracted.

And so had I when I'd swung the door closed. Now Christine opened it without a key.

"Hello?" she called. The dogs' collars clinked.

I stared down at the dead cop. If she walked in here, she would see it. I had no time to wrap any blankets around it or cover it with laundry.

"Hello?" she said again, louder, and I heard her step inside onto the linoleum. Entering someone else's house, not sure if it was empty, naturally made her pause then, and I knew I had to act fast to keep her in the other room.

"Just a second," I called back, and flicked off the light in my bedroom. The whole apartment was dark. I walked into the other room and pulled the bedroom door shut behind me.

"Hey," Christine said. "I thought you went out."

"No," I said. I flicked on the overhead light in my kitchenette. "I'm about to go out now."

"Did that cop come over here?" she asked.

"Oh, yeah," I said, as if she'd reminded me, "he wanted me to give you your keys back." I took her keys from my pocket and handed them to her.

"What did he say to you?"

I shrugged.

"Where did he go?" she asked.

"He said he wanted to go to the bar," I told her. "I don't know what bar he meant. I let him out the side door."

"He must have meant Cody's." She shook her head a little. "I gave him the keys so he could leave you a note, because you said you were going out. He just suddenly wanted to know about you. That's so bizarre."

"He asked me what I do and stuff," I said.

"Yeah, I told him you worked in the hardware store, and he was like, 'Let me go leave him a note with my card.'"

"He wanted to know if I knew about that other hardware store," I said. "That one near here on Broad."

"Isn't that where you work?"

"Oh, no!" I shook my head. "He's talking about that place right near here, where those people got killed."

"What people?"

"I don't know, it was on the news," I said. "Probably it was a robbery, I bet. Anyway, he wondered if I knew anything about those people, you know, since we both worked in hardware stores. But I didn't."

"So where's this store you work at?"

"I don't work there anymore," I corrected her. "Anyway, I've got to take the dogs out now."

For once her coke habit worked in my favor. She wouldn't have let me change the subject so abruptly had she not desperately wanted to return to that china plate under her bed.

She left. I watched her cross the yard. Inside I tingled, letting myself sense for the first time how close I had just come to chaos. It hadn't riled me, because I had deliberately ignored it. While talking to Christine I'd actually believed what I told her, that the cop had asked me a few questions and gone to the bar.

I found the cop's car keys in his hip pocket. The ignition key had a Ford symbol on it. The keyring hung by a chain from a black plastic box about an inch square and half an inch deep, its edges and corners rounded, a shiny black button in the middle of one side. After studying this little box a moment I decided it was the remote for the cop's car alarm; I'd seen people use them on TV shows, but nobody films closeups of the actual tool in an actor's hand. The Chrysler I'd driven down to New Orleans didn't have an alarm, which explains how it wound up stolen in the first place.

I took the dogs out again. We went around the block, past the bar. Since Cody had a crowd of customers tonight, all the parking spaces along the curb were filled. Over near Christine's house I looked for Fords and didn't find any. I didn't want to have to walk around trying the key in different cars.

Instead I pressed the alarm button. Nothing happened. We went back past the bar to the corner, and I pressed it again. Still no answer. I didn't know how far a range the remote should have, so I walked down my block, away from Cody's, pressing the button as I passed each car. Nothing happened.

Halfway down my block I paused. These people had all parked here because they'd come to the bar. Yet the cop had come to see Christine. He would've parked closer to her house. And in fact, I reasoned, if he'd come down Gentilly from the other direction, he would have just pulled over across the street, in front of the racetrack.

There were three cars parked over there. The dogs and I crossed Gentilly Boulevard, and when we reached the sidewalk I pressed the button. A piercing, high-pitched bwoowoop came from under the hood of a tan car, an El Torino. I unlocked the passenger door and held it open. Stupid jumped right in the back. Useless didn't want to, at first, but he finally followed, warily. As I climbed in behind the wheel I wondered why he distrusted cars, if maybe his owners might have ditched him on the highway.

I pulled a U-turn at the entrance to the racetrack and then drove around the block to my street. No one was around to see me, but that could change in a second, especially with the bar full right up the street. I parked close to the opposite corner, five or six houses down from mine.

The adventure of riding in the car satisfied the dogs enough that they climbed out and returned to the house with me willingly. Walking down the alley behind them I could see a bounce in their step.

As I pulled the key out, Stupid abruptly held dead still, listening to something inside the apartment. Useless looked at Stupid, then at the door.

I unlocked it quietly. For a second I stood there, wondering how to keep the dogs quiet. Once I opened the door, they would charge to the bedroom, and I'd left the bedroom door shut. And I'd left the gun in the cop's holster.

Every second I waited meant the cop could be inside, conscious again, getting ready for me. Really angry and scared. Positive he had to kill me on sight.

I held Stupid back by his collar and squeezed in through the door myself. I hated to leave my dogs in the alley, but neither one barked. My gun—the one I got from Wayne—was in my bedroom. I tried to think of anything I could use as a club, like a baseball bat. All that came to mind were gardening tools, for which I would have to go to the shed.

It began to seem as if standing there in the kitchenette would upset me, so I just threw the bedroom door open and stormed inside. The cop hadn't moved. I took his gun, and on second thought I took his ankle holster from him, too. Then I went and let the dogs in. They sat and watched me deal with the thing on my bedroom floor.

I didn't have any dropcloths. At last I decided to wrap it in my shower curtain. The bundle would look suspect to anyone who paid real attention, but all I needed to worry about were drunks coming out of Cody's. No one else would see me between my door and the El Torino.

The whole time I carried it there, the street was dead silent. No cars even passed behind me on Gentilly. In the cop's trunk I found an empty gasoline can. I took it out and left the package in its place.

A woman inside the bulletproof booth at the Chevron on Esplanade wanted to know why I wanted the gas in my can rather than my car. "You ain't supposed to do that," she told me.

"What, put gas in a gas can?" I asked.

"Not in your trunk," she said. "It's a fire hazard. It's illegal. Why don't you just put it in your tank?"

"Look," I began, and had to pause for a breath while I invented an explanation. "I borrowed this car from my wife's friend so I could get two bucks' worth. My own car ran out of gas and I pushed it home. My gas gauge is broken."

"Oh," she said, "all right."

"Yeah, I can see what you're saying, though," I said with a nod. She took my ten dollars. Probably I shouldn't have carried the can with me when I went to pay. This Chevron wasn't too busy at night, so the clerks had time to watch people. No doubt I should also have gone to a busier gas station, farther away, in case the cops came asking about me, but if the cops got their hands on a photo of me to show people, by that point it wouldn't matter much one way or the other whether this clerk remembered me.

From the gas station I drove into City Park. After a minute I changed my mind. Cops must patrol this place, I figured, and on these little wooded lanes it would prove impossible to hide. I did a three-point turn and came back out to the street, where I made a left onto Wizner Boulevard. I drove along the bayou, watching for secluded spots. The problem was that I needed to walk home afterward.

Finally I picked a glade not too far from a footbridge over the bayou. I drove the car underneath the canopy of a weeping beech. On the other side I found a small open patch, where the car fit with nothing much near it. I climbed out and walked around. It crossed my mind that I should have brought the dogs, in case a cop should stop me on the way out of here.

First I walked around a bit. From the road no one could see the El Torino through the trees, though that wouldn't matter much. I listened to frogs in the bayou. Something flew past me, hunting low over the water, probably a bat.

This glade was nice. I didn't like the idea of trashing the place, but I couldn't come up with another way to solve this particular dilemma. And I started to notice all the garbage on the grass, and in the bushes and everywhere else, fast food bags and beer bottles hurled from cars. The people who lived in this city didn't care at all about using a place this pretty as a dump. That made it a lot easier for me.

I poured gasoline all over the steering wheel and both door handles. Then I opened the trunk and drenched everything in there. I couldn't think of a way to leave a slow fuse burning that I knew for sure would ignite, so I just chucked a match in the window. The flames roared before I even left the glade.

Instantly the fire lit the area too well for me to run right along the side of the road. Someone might have stopped to help me, or cops might happen by. To hide I ran along the shoreline of the bayou. By dumb luck I made it to the footbridge without falling in.

On the other side of the bridge I found myself on De Saix Boulevard. I heard an explosion, which I assumed meant the car's fuel tank had blown. By the time I walked half a block more, sirens were squealing in the distance. My hands reeked of gas. I bent down to wipe them on someone's front lawn.

Soon two cop cars screamed past, headed for the fire. Neither noticed me. I kept walking, glancing down each cross street I passed. They were all dead ends. Then I reached Gentilly Boulevard, which surprised me because I had expected it to run perpendicular to De Saix. Something about the shape of New Orleans keeps the streets from forming any kind of reliable pattern, especially there by the racetrack.

Another uncommon aspect of New Orleans is how the city's concave shape distorts the sky overhead. As I walked home I saw lightning in the distance ahead of me; the heavens appeared actually lower at the horizon, as if people standing on their roofs a few miles away could touch the long, splintered shafts of light bursting above them. Dust in the atmosphere muted the lightning and tinted it red. No specific clap of thunder accompanied any one flash, but gradually my ears came to detect a constant metallic grinding up there.

Storms move rapidly across such a flat landscape, too. By the time I reached home, regular bluish-white lightning had flashed several times. Still it made no definite sound.

The backs of my knees ached, not from walking but from the aftermath of repeated adrenaline rushes. I wanted to bathe and sleep. Sex was the furthest thing from my mind now. But I needed to enter Christine's, because I had no bleach, which I would need to clean the blood off my bedroom wall and floor. She wouldn't notice if I swiped hers, so long as I put it back before she did her laundry.

So I dragged myself across the yard to see her.

"Where'd you go?" she asked me.

"Oh," I said, and waved the question away.

"Where?" she asked again.

Something in her manner didn't feel right to me, and it wasn't only the effects of the cocaine. I wondered whether she might have come looking for me again and found the dogs home.

"Huh?" she prodded me.

I kissed her and started taking her clothes off. The mood came back, just as easily as that.

Later, after we finished, she said, "Oh, yeah, are your dogs okay?"

"Okay how?"

"I think one of them hurt his snout," she said. "I petted them both when I saw you at your house before, and when I got home I found blood on my hand. See?" She held up a dish towel she'd used to wipe her hand. "I thought at first it was my blood, but I don't have any cuts."

I told her Stupid had bled a little from his mouth, because he was cutting teeth. That explained it. We went to sleep.

# 23

THE NEXT MORNING I SWIPED HER BLEACH and went home to clean my bedroom. Christine kept her laundry supplies in a shoulder bag tucked beside the wicker hamper in her bathroom.

The blood in my room had dried but it wiped off easily. I still had a half-can of paint from when I'd done the walls cameo white, so I covered the small area discolored by the bleach. Blood itself turns brown as it dries, yet the blotches left after scrubbing it can be all sorts of colors. For instance, it'll stain a porcelain tub yellow.

All morning I found myself growing anxious. Rather than start painting or mending the fence and then get distracted, I stayed inside with Christine. We watched nature shows. Around lunchtime I began to relax; if the police knew enough to ask her about what they found in Detective Holland's trunk, they would have called already.

It seemed to me that they would check the phone records on the dead cop's pager number, and that would lead them to Christine. She would tell them he had talked to me. When they talked to me I would have to appear helpful. Any mention of the hardware store could prove disastrous, I knew. The plan formed in my mind to say he had offered me yard work somewhere nearby, that I had turned him down. This story would conflict with what Christine would tell them, so I would say I lied to her out of embarrassment. The plan grew so far that I decided to say the neighborhood he asked me about was Lakeview, only I would pretend I couldn't remember the name exactly.

So I didn't doubt that I could survive any questions they might throw at me. But the idea of having to face possibly hostile cops—and smart ones, homicide guys with a lot of pressure on them to catch whoever had killed their friend—the whole idea of it hung over my head.

Around noon it stopped worrying me. Christine made tuna salad. While we ate, I saw my position more clearly, unblurred by fear: Probably the safest thing I could do would be to leave, which meant I needed somewhere to go. Texas has too many cops. The nearest place I could go was Florida.

Yet I wanted to stay. Moving the dogs would be a hassle. Christine would not want to go, either.

After lunch, she told me she would go job hunting in the Quarter again that afternoon. Something about the way she announced this journey struck me odd, as though she were hiding her real motives, but right then I just wanted her off my hands for a few hours. The morning had taken a toll on my nerves, and I wanted to be rested for what I needed to do that afternoon.

A little before three-thirty I showed up at that corner bar next to Balconis. The bartender had one other customer, an older man he seemed to know real well, and they two sat at the far end of the bar. I gave him five dollars for a coke and sat at a table that let me watch the sidewalk through the front window.

In about ten minutes Gary passed. On reflex I pulled away, worried he would spot me, but he didn't even glance into the bar. In fact, I believe he was talking to himself.

Across the street came a teenager who glanced around at the buildings, checking addresses. I left the bar and intercepted him just as he reached the front gate at Balconis.

"Excuse me," I said.

He faced me but didn't speak.

"Did Father LaSalle send you?"

Shaking his head, he said, "Father Murphy."

"Oh," I said. "I don't think I know him. Anyway, we don't need you today."

"Who doesn't?" the kid asked. "The restaurant?"

I nodded.

"Because I was hoping to make some money," the kid said. His eyes were rueful.

In my pocket I had fifty dollars ready. I pulled it out and handed it to him. "Do me a favor?" I said.

He listened to me obediently. Rather than surly he seemed just a little slow.

"Tell Father LaSalle or whoever it is that we don't need any more dishwashers," I said. "We have someone full-time now. Okay?"

Rather than listening to what I'd said, the kid had been searching his mental records for the correct priest's name. "I think I should tell Father Murphy," he said. "He gives out the jobs."

"Well, whoever it is over there," I told him.

"I'm pretty sure it's Father Murphy usually," he said. "But I could tell Father LaSalle, too. If you want."

"As long as they get the message."

The kid looked at me expectantly, and I knew he needed me to repeat what I wanted him to say: "We don't need any more dishwashers. We've got someone full-time."

"Gotcha," the kid said as he walked away.

"And tell them I said hi," I added.

The kid stopped and spun around, holding one ear a little forward to show he hadn't heard me.

"I said hi," I said. "Tell them I said hi."

"Who?"

"Father Murphy."

"I thought you didn't know him," the kid said.

"Tell him anyway." Before the kid could ask what my name was, I went inside the restaurant.

Jody was at the greet stand just inside the front door, though I didn't know yet that her name was Jody. She had hair the color of a brand-new penny. When she looked up at me, she knew instantly that I wasn't a customer.

"I'm here to wash dishes," I told her.

"Uhm," she replied, curious but not sure how to phrase what she wanted to ask.

"Father Murphy sent me."

"Oh." Her face relaxed, though the sight of me still puzzled her.

"I'm a friend of Father LaSalle's," I said. "They usually send kids, right?"

"Well, yeah," Jody said. "But that's all right."

"Yeah, I could use the money, and Father said, 'You want to do this?'" I told her. "I mean, you know. It's not always a good thing for kids to get their hands on money. I guess."

Jody introduced herself and led me down a hall to a back door. The kitchen was in the slave quarter, that separate building behind the cottage. As I followed I looked at her; she didn't dress to show off her body, but she didn't have to.

I didn't see Gary anywhere. We passed that back bar where I'd seen Chuck drinking. Standing there with a tumbler full of dark liquor was a man with gray hair and a face flush with color from booze. The way he stood showed that he thought he was in charge of something. I would learn later that his name was Don, and that in fact his wife Virginia supported him, largely by owning forty percent of Balconis.

"Have you ever worked in a kitchen?" Jody asked me as we crossed the patio.

"Sure have," I said. That was of course true. "Maybe not as fancy as this."

"All right, I'm going to tell you the worst part up front, just so you know," Jody said. "Standard kitchen rules, the dishwasher has to clean up if there are any accidents. That includes if anybody throws up, okay?"

"Okay," I said.

"It hardly ever happens here," she said, "but when it does I can't stand to have to argue with someone. So you know in advance." She opened the door to the kitchen and held it for me, then added, "I don't like making someone do something I wouldn't do myself."

"That's all right," I told her. Just from meeting her, I felt that she shouldn't have to clean up someone's puke. Anyway, I'd done that before, too.

The chef was a tall woman who looked friendly but tired. Even the burn scars on her forearms added to this effect. Everyone just called her Chef, rather than by her name. Two other cooks worked with her, a girl in her twenties who was assistant chef and a middle-aged man who just prepared food before the others cooked it. All three shook my hand and resumed ignoring me.

The washer had a small pantry all to itself. This machine worked basically the same as the one they forced me to learn when I was a teenager. (Gardening jobs were the hardest to get; I had to wait two years working in the kitchen and the laundry.) It was a metal cube three foot wide, on top of a counter as high as my waist. I had to arrange the dishes on a square plastic rack, slide the rack along the counter into the washer, then pull the sides of the cube down. That automatically triggered the wash cycle. Two minutes later the sides would pop up, and I would slide the rack out the other side, where most of the dishes would dry on their own due to the heat of the water.

Aside from running the washer, I only had to scrape food off the plates into the garbage and stack the dry dishes in the kitchen proper for the chefs to use. The busboys—they wore ties and called themselves "back waiters"—brought all the dirty plates from the dining room. Compared to other kitchen experiences of mine, this was pretty light.

The cooks didn't chat while they worked. Instead they kept the radio on, tuned to a station that only played old songs. The DJ introduced a lot of them as New Orleans records from before I was born, but others I knew from when I was a kid. I even heard a song called "Brandy" by Looking Glass, which I only know because someone gave me that forty-five for my birthday. I don't know as much about rock music as most people my age.

A door on the side of the little pantry opened onto an alley, hidden from both the patio and restaurant. The waiters came back here to take their cigarette breaks. No one knew or cared that I could hear their gossip. For all anyone but Jody and the cooks could tell, I didn't speak English. After your first ten years under supervision, playing dumb becomes a mask you wear all the time.

Early in the evening Jody's name caught my ear out in the alleyway. A girl laughed and said someone named Far China was making Jody's life difficult.

Later Chef left her underlings running the kitchen. From then on, the staff took more and longer smoke breaks. They also began coming out two or three at a time, which increased the conversation. Personally I thought these people spent more time than necessary in the alley.

Gary didn't recognize me. Without really looking he marched right past me to join a waiter and a waitress already smoking. They chatted about a bar they all liked. Their voices blurred behind me until at one point Gary said, "He's killing Anna. Just fucking killing her."

The other two shushed him. The waitress crept forward to make sure Chef couldn't hear them, as if she didn't know Chef had left the kitchen.

"I don't know anything about it," the other guy said. "It's none of my business."

"Yeah, well, it's *my* business," Gary said. "I've been friends with them a long time. This is fucking ridiculous. And it's a shitty spot to put Chef in. That's all I'm saying."

The other two went back to work, leaving Gary to finish his cigarette. Still he didn't recognize me. I felt sure that if I didn't speak to him, he'd never look twice at me in the corner there, washing dishes. Balconis went through a lot of dishwashers, it seemed like.

Toward the end of the night Jody came out. That's when I realized who "Far China" was: The staff called Virginia "Vargina." They also called her husband "Dong." Virginia was Terry's mother-in-law, the woman Gary had told me about the first night I met him. She insisted on overseeing everyone's work while drinking on her medication. Apparently no one could tell her no.

"She's such a fucking mess," Jody snarled. She held the tips of her thumb and her index finger half an inch apart. "I'm this close to saying, 'Virginia, did you invest in a restaurant so you and your asshole third husband could come get drunk here and prevent us from doing business smoothly?' You know? He sits in there, boozing and telling his life story to customers in the bar—"

"Oh, I *know*," a waiter told Jody. "The other night, when you were off? Oh, my God." He waved both his hands, as if overwhelmed. "There's this young couple—they're from, like, Cleveland or someplace. Dong starts talking to them in the bar while they're waiting to be seated. Then after they've got a table, he comes traipsing in with his drink and sits down with them. While they're eating."

"You're kidding," Jody said.

"It was my table," he said.

"Did they care?" Jody asked.

"*Yeah*, they fucking cared. They're like twenty-nine, and they've got this obnoxious old souse pulling up a chair at their table. And it's like *I've* got to get rid of him, you know?"

"Oh, I know," she said.

"Because, I mean, you shouldn't have to chase someone away like that."

"Oh, totally," Jody agreed. "Plus, if they don't have as good a time, there goes your tip."

The guy dropped his cigarette, ground it out with his shoe. "No, they tipped me all right. I was going to say something to Chef, but what's the point?"

"She won't do shit," Jody said, shaking her head.

"She can't."

"She could," Jody corrected him. "Chef could tell them to get out of our way. Vargina isn't the boss."

A little more quietly, the guy asked, "Do they have any other investments?"

"*He* doesn't have *anything*," Jody said, a faint hiss in her voice. "Don wouldn't own a pair of fucking socks if he didn't marry Virginia. She inherited money, and I think she got some from her first husband."

"Terry's wife's father."

"Right." Jody stamped out her smoke, too. They went back inside. I peeked at her as she passed me.

At the end of the night Jody paid me forty dollars cash. The assistant chef gave me a chicken dinner in a closed styrofoam tray to take home. When I asked Jody if I could work the next night too, she shrugged and told me to show up the same time.

# 24

I slept over Christine's that night. She didn't get high but acted cranky anyway, probably from getting high the night before. Cocaine changes your brain chemistry, and it takes a few days for your brain to change back. Don't bother telling that to someone who uses the stuff.

Nine-thirty the next morning I raided Tara's mailbox again. Nothing in there would cheer up Ennis.

Outside the post office I walked back toward that copy shop. On the way I stopped at a payphone in front of a dingy bar to call Ennis collect at his job.

"What's up?" he asked.

"The man she's seeing is in his mid-fifties," I told Ennis. "Everyone who knows him says he's a scumbag."

"How do you know this?"

"His family owns a restaurant in the Quarter," I explained. "He brings Tara there in front of his wife's friends. He's talking to Tara about marriage, I think."

"Wait, wait, wait," Ennis said. "Where did you get all this?"

I explained about the letter and that I had a job now at Balconis. Ennis took the news about Tara well, probably because he couldn't throw a fit at work. I had him give me his fax number so I could send him Tara's phone bill and Chuck's letter. Ennis declared himself pleased with my "work."

After we hung up I went inside the copy store and sent him the documents. For just a flash the girl behind the counter glanced at one of the sheets as she arranged them in the machine. If she suspected anything odd, though, she forgot it by the time she helped the next customer.

When the fax had gone through she handed the copies back to me along with a sheet of printed confirmation, all of which I ripped into quarters and chucked in a recycling bin near the door.

That left me with about four or five hours to kill. Painting the fence back home didn't appeal to me that day. Neither did seeing Christine, though she might go job-hunting again in the afternoon.

I sat in that park across the street from the post office. The homeless men didn't come ask me for money, maybe because so many better-dressed people now walked past the park on both Saint Charles Avenue and Camp Street. I noticed how the women in this business district preferred out-of-date hairstyles.

A young girl pulled a light-blue convertible into an illegal parking space and hopped out of her car. As she dashed up the steps to the post office she glanced around for meter maids or cops. Not until she had run inside did I realize it was Tara.

Very soon she came back out carrying her mail and climbed into her car. When she looked my way I turned to watch a streetcar full of tourists for a few seconds, then looked back.

Tara still had her eyes on me, as if trying to place me. But I had my sunglasses on and my hair cut much shorter than when Ennis had introduced us. As she pulled out, she peeked at me once more, supposedly by accident. Since I was now meeting her stare, she immediately looked away and drove off.

It didn't worry me. Even if by some chance she could recall seeing me with Gary through the window at Balconis, driving in midday traffic for a minute or two would wipe this whole moment from her mind.

Mostly the sight of Tara made me wonder about Ennis. This girl didn't love him anymore, if she ever had. Her life had grown away from his and she wanted it that way. The only thing I knew about her that I liked was that she'd been close with her dog.

A little while later I left the park. A few blocks away I found the main library, so I went in and read a book about alligators, and then an article about training dogs to work with handicapped people. A number of people sitting at the tables in this library carried lots of belongings with them in plastic shopping bags. They smelled bad, too, but more from wearing too-heavy clothes in sunny weather than from living outdoors.

Around two I left the library, in search of food. I found a lunch place nearby that served the corporate crowd. They had pretty decent hamburgers. After I ate I thought about going back to the library but didn't really feel like it.

I arrived at Balconis an hour early. A man of about thirty-five stood at the greet stand as I entered. When he saw my workshirt his eyes narrowed just a tiny bit.

"Hi, I'm here to wash dishes," I said.

For a moment he blinked at me, then he checked his watch and said, "Oh. You're early."

"Yeah, sorry," I said. "Jody just told me to come back if I wanted to do it again today. I didn't want to be late."

"No, that's fine," he said, and stuck out his hand. "I'm Terry."

I shook his hand and introduced myself. He suggested I go sit on the patio until four. "It's nice out there," he said.

Though the end of the lunch crowd still had their tables inside the restaurant, there were no customers left out back. For a moment I thought I had the whole patio to myself, but then I spotted Jody at a table behind some kind of fern plant. She sat reading a black hardcover book, resting her chin upon one hand.

"Hey," I said.

"How are you?" she greeted me, and smiled.

"I'm early."

"So I see," Jody said. "Sit down."

I did, and she showed me her book, which was a novel with the word hummingbird in the title. Reading has always provided direct and useful information in my life, so I have never read novels. I admire people who do.

Jody lit a cigarette. She offered me one, but I don't smoke. Mostly we talked about the restaurant, since I didn't feel like lying to her about my own life and I couldn't get her to talk about hers, other than that she'd come from Illinois a year ago with a fellow she no longer spoke to.

A lot of celebrities ate at Balconis, hardly any of them people I'd heard of. I don't watch TV or follow sports. Yet it excited Jody to talk about these guys, so I smiled and nodded. A few times I said, "Really?"

Sitting there, feeling her smile at me, I had a flash that I could actually be myself around this girl. For a time I had no idea what words came out of my mouth or hers and it didn't matter. I didn't have to care what we told each other. Never before had I felt that way, ever. It put me into a kind of shock, I think.

Chef left even earlier than she had the previous night. It wasn't dark yet when Jody came back for her first smoke break. She had her teeth gritted when she passed me, so I didn't mind her ignoring me.

"I'd like to fucking kill that cunt," Jody said to that same guy she'd been talking to yesterday.

"Don't let her get you all—"

"It's too late," Jody said. "I'm already pissed. She goes to me, 'When you're older, you'll understand.'"

"About what?"

"About Chuck," Jody said, spitting his name out. "Gary told Chuck's wife about titty girl, whatever her name is, and Chuck's all bent out of shape about it."

"What's that got to do with you?" the guy asked.

"I know, right?" Jody told him. "But then he complains to Chef that I'm meddling. As if I even care. He calls up for his table and he goes, 'Can I speak to Virginia, please? This is Fred.' Like I don't know his voice. So I go, 'Just a second, Chuck.' And he gives Virginia shit about it."

"Great! Let him," the waiter said. "Let him complain his little heart out. I think you're holding all aces this hand, Jody. Let him talk to Virginia all day."

"Yeah, no shit, but then I've got Vargina—when I'm trying to do the reservation book, no less, which she has drunkenly fucked up yet again—she starts giving me this lecture about how I should treat Chuck, blah blah blah, and she goes, 'When you're older, honey, you'll understand.' You know? I'm thirty-two years old, I'm not some fucking teenager she can say that to."

"That is..." He shook his head, exhaling smoke. "That's fucked up. On every level."

"I mean it, next time when he brings his little whore in here, I should punch her right in the tits," Jody said, and burst out laughing. She had the nicest laugh. She really meant it.

On the radio I heard "Dream Weaver," by someone with the last name Wright. In my mind I could see the gray-and-pink label of the forty-five, but I couldn't recall the guy's first name. The DJ on this station only talked about a record if someone from New Orleans made it.

An hour or so later Gary came out and talked about Chuck some more, though he didn't seem as outraged as usual. He and a waitress I hadn't seen before traded gossip about Tara. From what they said I gathered that the first time Tara met Chuck at Balconis for lunch, she arrived in her work clothes, including that long, scuzzy wig. Afterward Virginia spoke to Chef, who then had a talk with Chuck. Now Tara came here wearing normal clothes rather than "babydoll" dresses (by which I assumed the waitress meant the juvenile getup I saw Tara strip out of at the club). Evidently Virginia felt she had to kiss Chuck's ass because Chef would soon have the opportunity to buy back Virginia's share of Balconis, and Virginia didn't want that to happen.

At one point, talking about Tara, this waitress said, "Supposedly she went to Tulane on a scholarship for French."

Gary shook his head and told her, "No, not French. It was..." For a moment he stared down the alley, puffing his cigarette. Then he shrugged and gave up. "I can't think of it. It wasn't French, though. Chuck was bragging about it the other night to Terry."

"In front of you?"

"Oh, no," Gary said with a laugh. "No, Chuck is steering clear of me."

She asked him something too softly for me to hear, and they continued speaking quietly. Odd they should lower their voices, since they obviously didn't know I could hear them. When they both finished their cigarettes, I wondered what subject these two felt the need to hide from unseen ears. Their bosses' private lives and finances hadn't required such secrecy.

About half an hour after the last entrees went out, Jody came into the pantry to tell me some woman had puked in the ladies' bathroom.

"I'm sorry," Jody told me. "You have to clean it."

"That's all right," I said. "It's not your fault."

A paunchy woman at least sixty years old pushed through the kitchen door and lost her balance, just slightly. At once I thought this was the culprit, barging into the kitchen to finish vomiting. But she nodded hello to the assistant chef and came to the pantry door.

"I've taken care of it," Jody said to this woman.

The woman addressed me as if she hadn't heard. She spoke in that starchy, blithering manner that alcoholic matrons use when they want to sound grave. "We have a problem inside," Virginia began.

"I told him," Jody said.

Virginia placed her hands up, palms forward, to interrupt Jody as though some important point needed to be made. "Unfortunately, one of the guests has taken ill..."

"I know," I said. "Where's the mop?"

"...I would not ask you to do this, except..."

"I know," I said again. "It's the dishwasher's job."

Jody stormed out of the kitchen, grinding her jaws. Virginia didn't notice; instead she drew a breath and told me, "The way to handle this is quickly and quietly."

"Of course. Just show me where the mop and the bucket are," I said, smiling at her. "I'm Louis, by the way," I added, sticking out my hand.

Virginia didn't want to shake it.

✲ ✲ ✲

Don came and talked to me while I worked, mostly about himself and places he'd traveled. Then, in a whisper that customers at their tables could overhear, he offered me a drink in the bar once I finished.

"Thanks," I said. "I don't drink."

"You sure? We have some excellent tequilas."

I pictured myself dumping the bucket of vomit over his head while shouting, "*You* don't have *shit*, you mooch."

Fantasies of that kind present a very real danger for me, so I shouldn't indulge them. I only broke my rule because of Jody. I knew that, too. Every time I saw her eyes glint with anger beneath those copper bangs, my heart moaned inside me.

Not long after I cleaned the bathroom, the assistant chef handed me my dinner and Jody paid me. She gave me fifty bucks instead of forty. "I'm sorry about Virginia," Jody said, rolling her eyes. "What a drunk slag that woman is."

"Didn't make any difference to me. She gets on your nerves, I can tell," I said.

"Tell me about it."

I went home in a cab. The dogs needed to go outside right away, so I ate in the yard, carrying the styrofoam container around with me. For dinner the kitchen had given me a fish filet on top of noodles with some kind of garlic sauce. Food from Balconis didn't taste like the other stuff I'd had in Louisiana. It was more like fancy Italian.

Christine's lights were on, so I unlocked her kitchen door and walked inside. Right away I knew she had scored coke again. The house just felt that way. Sure enough, when I reached her living room she had the plate loaded on her coffee table. She didn't even try to hide it.

"Hey," she said, without taking her eyes from the television.

I held the container out to her. "Want some dinner?"

She shook her head. "Where'd you get that?"

"At work."

"Where do you work, again?" she asked me.

"A restaurant."

"What's it called?"

I looked at the ceiling. "I can't think of the name... It's in the French Quarter."

"Where, on Decatur Street?"

"I think it's near Decatur Street," I said, and then I got her to describe the Quarter to me, which distracted her from figuring out what restaurant I worked at.

After a few minutes of geography, she asked me outright if I felt like fucking her. I didn't really, especially since she put it that way, but I knew better than to say so. I told her that first I needed to put the dogs back in my house and feed them. Christine received this news with a slow nod of her head.

Outside I stared at the sky for a long time. When I looked down, I found the dogs had sat beside me and looked upward too, trying to see whatever I was staring at.

I had to go fuck Christine. Not like it was any big chore, but my mood wouldn't put up with a lot tonight. If she played games, I might get upset. In a way meeting Jody had triggered this fear, since I could tell I wouldn't have half the problems with her that Christine gave me.

# 25

I SPENT THE NEXT MORNING IN THE YARD WITH MY DOGS. Useless woke up a little sluggish, so I checked him over. First I pressed my fingers on the inside upper part of his hind leg, until I found his heartbeat. It seemed weak, but I had never checked it before, so I couldn't tell if that was normal. Stupid's pulse was much stronger, but the difference might just reflect their ages.

Next I peeled back Useless's upper lip and squeezed his gum until it turned white. I counted from one-thousand-one until one-thousand-three before his gum turned pink again. It should have been quicker, but I couldn't remember what condition that symptom signified. Shock seemed most likely, since I'd learned this trick when I was a kid as part of pet first aid.

Around one o'clock the mailman made Pat sign for an overnight package from Ennis, which Pat then brought back to me. Inside it I found two hundred dollars in twenties and a typed note, unsigned.

Ennis wanted Chuck's license plate number. I had ideas of my own.

The phone book listed Chuck's address in Lakeview. I didn't recognize the name of his street, so I didn't know any others it might intersect.

Rather than use Christine's phone to call a cab, I walked to the cab dispatch on Gentilly. This way, if for some reason someone asked the driver later where he picked me up, it wouldn't matter.

In my breast pocket I had Wayne's parcel of cocaine. The revolver I carried in a paper bag. The dispatcher made a joke about the bag, something about sharing my lunch. He had too thick an accent for me to decipher exactly what he said. I just smiled at him.

In a few minutes a black driver picked me up. He drove a big cab that felt old, like an early '70s car someone has reupholstered and painted while letting rust eat the chassis. The man drove with his left hand and kept his right arm stretched along the top of the seat next to him, as if holding an invisible girlfriend.

"Where you going, now?" the driver asked as we went up Gentilly to De Saix.

"Lakeview," I said.

"Where in Lakeview?"

I pretended I didn't remember the house number, but I assured him I would recognize the house because I'd been there before. We got to Chuck's neighborhood quickly, and right away I could see I'd made a mistake bringing Wayne's stuff here now. No way could I slip into their yard unseen. People were everywhere. I would need instead to come back early in the morning, when everyone would be leaving for work or sleeping. Also, I didn't know whether Anna worked. If not, I would have to come on a morning when she left the house for an hour or two, time enough for me to find the right place to "hide" the gun and coke so she could find them.

But at least now I knew right where their house was.

"Oh, damn!" I said, and patted my shirt pockets as though looking for something.

"What's the matter?" the driver asked me.

"I forgot something at work," I told him. "You know what? I need to go back to the French Quarter."

The cabbie brought me downtown. The trip took fifteen minutes. I gave him a big tip and got out on Burgundy in front of a grocery three blocks from Balconis. He asked me if I needed him to take me back to Lakeview. I shook my head. Until he drove off I didn't understand what he meant, that he believed my story about coming here to retrieve something from my job.

As I walked to the restaurant it dawned on me that I was still carrying Wayne's gun. I'd grown used to the paper sack in my hand, forgetting that if anyone saw what I had in there, I could expect the police in seconds. It didn't matter—since I would stash the sack under the dishwasher without anyone's knowing, then take it home with me in a cab—but it showed me how blithe and careless I'd become. It would not have happened had I stayed out of New Orleans.

I had my sunglasses on, so as I came down the alley toward the door I could stare inside the window without anyone's noticing. Tara and Chuck were sitting at "his" table. For a long moment I stopped, facing dead ahead at the courtyard, pretending I'd suddenly remembered an errand I needed to run. While I stood there I kept my eyes on Tara. My life had become entangled with hers, after we had met for a minute or so, by accident. As she sat there listening to Chuck she smiled, just a little. Something about her made it difficult to watch, maybe because Chuck was so much older than she, and so sleazy-looking. It made me cringe.

When I went inside, Chef suggested I eat before working. She asked if I liked salmon, which I hadn't tried, and she handed me probably the best meal of my life, which I ate in the courtyard. I had never tasted sprouts before; they had become a common food while I was away. Whenever I'd heard anyone mention them, I'd pictured brussel sprouts. But these sprouts they served at Balconis looked like newly hatched grass seeds. The salmon just melted on my tongue.

So I settled in at the dishwasher half an hour later with my spirits high, though I felt just a little sleepy at first with my stomach so full. It made everything slow and comfortable, like in a dull dream. I laid the bag with the gun on the floor of the open locker where they kept the aprons.

The first hour passed quickly. A tall waitress I didn't know came to the back door for a smoke. Gary followed a little later. The waitress brought up Chuck and Tara, but for once Gary didn't want to talk about them. Instead he complained about living in a neighborhood called Kenner. Then they were joined by the girl whom I had heard trading gossip with Gary the day before. The other waitress greeted her by name, which sounded to me like Dana.

"Did you see the ensemble today?" Dana asked, excited.

"Oh," Gary told her, "I'm just, just—"

"Over it?" Dana suggested.

"No, I'm—well, maybe. Yeah, I'm over it." Gary stamped his cigarette out, even though he couldn't have been half finished yet. "I'm just so sick of Chuck, I can't even enjoy bad-mouthing him. He's just fucking pathetic."

Gary went back to work. The other two joked about Tara's clothes. They called her Little Orphan Annie, which didn't make a lot of sense to me because Tara didn't resemble the cartoon character at all. Probably they just meant to ridicule the way Tara made herself resemble a kid. Little Bo Peep would have worked better.

Around eight o'clock I left the kitchen so I could use the men's room. In the back hall I passed Virginia and Jody talking. The first thing I heard Virginia say was, "And that's how it is. I'm sorry, I don't have to change how I run things. It's my restaurant."

"It's *my* workplace," Jody said. "He's making me—"

"You don't have to work here," Virginia told her.

"Virginia, he's making me uncomfortable and I'm just doing my job," Jody said. "That's harassment. If you would just stay out of it—"

"No! You don't tell me that." Vargina looked really peeved. "I pay your salary. I'm telling *you* to stay out of it."

Jody's lips quivered as if she might cry. "*He* involved me in it! He calls up and pretends to be someone else! Like I give a shit that he cheats on his wife. And you talk to me like *I'm* the problem."

"You *are* the problem," Virginia said. "Your attitude is the problem."

"Oh, bullshit."

"Lower your voice," Virginia said.

I went into the bathroom. From inside I could still hear the two women arguing, but the closed door muffled whatever actual words they said. When I finished washing my hands, I rinsed my face with cool water. The mirror over the sink was very slightly concave, so that my face blinked back at me with my upper forehead subtly stretched and my eyes compressed just enough to make my anger more sad.

I stared until all feeling vanished. No matter what Virginia said to her, I couldn't show any interest. For one thing, it wouldn't impress Jody. You would think compassion like that would appeal to women, but they can take it funny. So I convinced myself it didn't matter to me.

When I came back out, Virginia was talking too low for me to hear. Jody stared at the floor and nodded slowly. I passed them without listening.

I couldn't say why, but when I reached the swinging doors to the kitchen I stood still. That's a dumb place to do that, since waiters push food out through those doors without warning. But there I was. My heart pounded in my ears. I suddenly could feel the effort it takes me every second to keep calm. This was not the first time I'd sensed that.

Somebody staggered into my peripheral vision on the left. I glanced up and saw Don, his face red, his eyes pink. He waved for me to follow him and walked into the bar. It seemed strange, so at first I stayed where I was. Then I followed. There were no customers waiting in there. Don stood in the middle of the room, hands on his hips.

Just as I caught up with him, Virginia called out from behind me, "Don, no."

He held up a hand to silence her. With a stern wobble of his head he said to me, "I want a word with you."

Virginia raised her voice and said, "Don, I'll talk to him. Later. Not now."

Don ignored her. So did I. I asked him, "What do you want to talk about, Don?"

"I'd like to know," he said, clumsily folding his arms, "why you told Covenant House we don't want any more dishwashers."

Right then I should have asked who Covenant House was, but I didn't think to. Instead I just held still. Angry heat flamed up the back of my neck.

"You don't have this job permanently," Don informed me. "You have no business telling Father LaSalle anything. We've had this agreement with them for years. You're way out of line."

"I've never heard of Father LaSalle," I lied, too late.

Don put his hand up again to stop me. "Bullshit," he said, almost but not quite sneering. "Jody spoke to him on the phone, and the kid who brought him the message saw the name Whitey on your shirt."

Which made it twice that same shirt had gotten me into trouble. I turned to look at Virginia. Jody stood two steps behind her, studying the carpet, ashamed to look at me. Virginia only met my gaze for an instant. Don had her full attention, probably because he was a lot drunker than she was just then.

But Jody wouldn't even glance at me. That did it.

"My name isn't Whitey," I told Don, evenly.

"Jody says she saw that name on the shirt you wore that day," Don said. He seemed to think he wielded great power in this situation. His mouth tightened into a grin that he intended to provoke me.

"Jody said that?" I asked.

"Mm-hmm," Don replied, moving his head up and down slowly, deliberately.

"She also says you should find somewhere else to get drunk, so you stop annoying the customers," I told him, speaking much faster than I wanted to. "It's not even your restaurant. Jody says you wouldn't own a pair of socks without Virginia."

Behind me I heard Virginia and Jody both gasp.

The ends of Dons eyebrows reached way up his forehead. "You're fired," he snapped.

I belted him in the mouth with my right fist. The knuckle of my middle finger made something inside his face give way, something half an inch too high up to be a tooth.

Don reeled backwards and landed across a small table where customers would sit with their drinks while waiting for their table in the restaurant. Until Don's head hit it I hadn't realized the table top was made of glass.

Once I heard it crash, everything became very loud to me, very frantic, impossible to understand.

Someone lunged at me from behind. I thrust my arm back, hard. Before I knew it, I had stabbed my elbow into Virginia's nose and knocked her to the floor with blood all over her face, a lot of blood. By this point I was yelling, I'm pretty sure.

I hadn't even realized Terry was still in the restaurant. He must have stayed after he got off work. I looked up just in time to see him charge me. It was a stupid thing to do, but he wasn't thinking. Terry was upset. Because of his mother-in-law, he acted like a crazed lunatic. I had to defend myself.

He managed to tackle me to the floor. We rolled. I couldn't draw my arm back far enough to punch him. He kicked over a stool from the bar. Then I grabbed his head and twisted it all the way around, until he whimpered and his neck snapped.

I stood up. Terry kept twitching. I beat him with the bar stool until it broke. When I finally calmed down, I found a sharp fifteen-inch spear from one of the stool's legs clenched in my hand.

The pressure inside me stopped. The whole building fell very quiet.

The bartender, the bar back, more than a dozen people who'd risen from their seats in the restaurant to come watch—nobody came near me. No one said a word. Jody had backed up to the wall with a hand over her mouth, but other than that she hadn't moved.

"You!" I said, pointing the stick at Jody.

She bolted out the door to the courtyard.

"If you didn't tell them, this wouldn't have happened," I told her, very loud but not shouting.

Far back in the crowd facing me from the restaurant, I saw Tara. She stood near Chuck as though for protection. She squinted at me. This time she knew my face.

I marched forward, and everyone between me and the kitchen doors cleared out of my way.

Chef had no idea what had just happened in the bar. When I walked past her she was chopping garlic while singing along to "The Night the Lights Went Out in Georgia."

In the pantry I untied my apron, took my bag from the locker, and charged out the back door. No one was on smoke break. I ran down the alley. At the far end another door led to the street. To open it I had to press a bar that said WARNING! ALARM WILL SOUND. And it did.

# 26

Where they kept me when I was sixteen, they didn't offer Driver's Ed. Much later I learned to drive by watching and imitating people. Getting pulled over meant getting sent away again, so I always drove very carefully, never running a red light or speeding. I tried to get a learner's permit once, but the woman giving the written test didn't believe that the birth certificate I showed her was mine.

There were still a few last minutes of twilight left when I reached the sidewalk outside Balconis. The alarm from the door grew fainter as I ran down Burgundy and turned the corner onto Saint Peter. Probably no one in the restaurant connected the noise to me yet, since they only saw me storm into the kitchen. But I couldn't take time to think about any of that. I needed to get out of the Quarter. The police could arrive any second.

A convertible sportscar passed me and pulled into a space halfway up the block. By the time I reached the car, the driver had opened his door.

I yanked Wayne's .38 from the paper bag and aimed it at the driver. He was a few years older than I and obviously had money. His eyes flared at the sight of the gun. He held both his hands up and climbed out from behind the wheel.

"Easy," he said, very calm. "What do you need, money?"

"Get away from the car," I told him.

"Okay." He still had his car keys in one of his hands.

"Drop the keys," I said. "Onto the seat."

"Wait. You don't want to steal this car—"

"Drop the keys!"

He did, but he kept talking. "This isn't a good car to steal," he explained, as if he knew all about fencing cars and I was some idiot who needed advice.

As soon as he got ten feet from the car I jumped in and closed the door. I slipped the square key into the ignition.

The car was a stickshift.

For a second there, I gave up. This car's owner had just gone for help, I had to assume, and I would not be able to drive away. Where could I run? But then I looked to my left. The man was still there, watching me.

I lowered the window and said, "How do I get this thing to go? Just to get it into gear."

"You don't know how to drive a standard?" He sounded incredulous. "If you can't drive it, don't ch—"

"I can drive! Just tell me how to start it and get in gear."

"Look, if you can't drive a standard, this is not the car to learn on."

I pointed the gun at his face. He kept talking without even flinching. "I'll give you money," he told me. "You can take a cab."

"I don't want to take a cab," I said. "How do I start the car?" I laid the gun on the seat beside me and turned the key. Nothing happened.

"I rebuilt that transmission myself," the man said, panic building in his voice. "Please. I'll do whatever you want. Just don't fuck up my transmission."

I picked up the revolver again. Still he didn't back away.

And then the man turned to his right. Again he raised both hands in the air. This time he waved his arms.

A second later he had flagged down another car.

I jumped out and ran to the driver's window. The blonde girl driving started to ask me what was wrong, but she stopped talking when I aimed Wayne's gun at her. She scrambled out. I didn't have to tell her to leave the keys.

This was a newer car but less fancy. At first glimpse I thought it was another standard, because the gearshift was between the driver and passenger seats. So it relieved me to see a little plastic window beside it with the letters P, N, R and D. The girl had put it into Park when the man stopped her, so I just had to shift into Drive and leave.

But the stick wouldn't change gears.

I tugged it, rattled it, shoved it both ways. Nothing. The car would not move.

Very probably the only reason I didn't become upset at this point was that I'd completely lost my mind not five minutes earlier. I just lacked the energy.

Outside the car, the man was now talking to the girl, explaining that he didn't know me, that I had just accosted him at gunpoint only seconds ago. I didn't have to hear exactly how he phrased it.

"So you pull me over for him to steal *my* car?" the girl sobbed.

He went on soothing her in that irritating helpful tone. If I listened, I would shoot him.

The knob on top of the gearshift had a small chrome button sticking out the side, right where your thumb would go. I pressed it and the stick moved.

Just as I shifted gears, the blonde girl punched the man in the face. Her fist clapped his eyesocket, making a sound like two billiard balls smacking. The guy fell, though maybe only for a second. I couldn't stick around to see how soon he got up.


As I drove home no one paid me any attention. To anyone watching me pass on Esplanade Avenue, I was just some fellow zipping home from work with a lot on his mind. A block before Claiborne, I put on my headlights. The dark fell fast now. Everything came crystal clear to me as I drove: I had to leave. And Christine could not come.

Though it was the last "cash only" city in America, New Orleans turned out to be a bad place to hide. I needed to go somewhere around people who kept their distance. As long as outsiders could push their way into my life, they could find out too much about me. Also, I needed to be careful about getting upset.

Christine did not have a place around me. I must have been crazy to fall in love. And I thought of the night she'd come into my house while that detective lay dead on my floor. If she'd taken a few steps forward and entered my bedroom, I would have killed her. It wasn't as if I didn't know it could happen.

It wasn't just the danger to her, either. As I drove up Bayou Road I thought of a house I'd seen the day before I reached New Orleans. On this house's roof stood a weathervane, the black iron kind that looks like a rooster and spins to show which way the wind blows. On this roof, though, it didn't spin anymore. Some kind of creeping vine had overgrown the house, and like barbed wire it held the rooster dead still. The sight of this thing had really disturbed me when I saw it; I had slowed the Chrysler down so I could see better.

What came to me as I drove home from Balconis was that the vines hadn't just sprouted there on that roof. They had climbed there, inch by inch. And on instinct they had seized the weathervane, maybe over the course of years. As long as the black bird could turn, the vines could not grab it. But one day the wind returned after a still week or month to find the tendrils fixed upon the rooster's claws strongly enough to resist. All things grow until they interfere.

And I began to think about the hospital. Or, actually, about Yusef's jacket. He had a suit they let him keep in his closet, but we couldn't have closets with doors. So I always saw this suit hanging in his room. Over time it came apart. You get used to seeing things fray and weather in a place like that. But now I wondered exactly when it became shabby. Which was the one loose thread too many?

My options were dwindling. I needed to think. I also needed a new set of papers, but the only source I knew for ID was far away and would probably prove useless now that I'd racked up a murder warrant as Louis Collins. Somewhere in Florida, inland away from the beaches where no one paid attention, I could lie low.

I pulled the car into the space directly in front of my house and went inside. One of the dogs had shat in the kitchen but I didn't bother to clean it. Since I couldn't tell which one hadn't gone, I let them both out my back door into the yard.

When they realized I wasn't coming out with them, both dogs moped at the bottom of the steps, uncertainly. "Go run around," I told them. "Go ahead."

Stupid trotted a short way into the yard. Useless stayed where he was, still hoping I'd come out. Once I walked away from the door, I knew, he might decide to follow me back inside.

I left the door slightly ajar so he could push it open if he wanted. First I needed to take a shower. All at once I felt very safe here. No one at Balconis had any idea where I lived, although by now they had to know I didn't stay at Covenant House. No one anywhere knew where to find me. Except Christine.

As I began to undress, I glanced down at a shirt on my floor and saw the Whitey nametag. This shirt had to go. My first thought was to burn it, but it didn't make sense to throw away a whole shirt when only the Whitey part was a problem.

In my bathroom cabinet I found a sewing needle, which I then used to break the thread along the edge of the nametag. As I worked the needle underneath the fifth or sixth loop, I noticed how tired I felt. A nagging fatigue had set in after I left the restaurant. Until getting home I'd had to ignore it. Unfastening this cloth patch from my shirt became a huge task.

I didn't move or say anything when I heard Useless push open the door from the yard. I held perfectly still in front of the mirror, prying the needle outward with my thumb to snap the thread.

In the kitchen, the floor creaked.

Neither dog weighed enough to make the floor creak.

I laid the needle on the sink and walked across the bedroom to look in the kitchen. Earlier I had used up my reserves of adrenaline, so now my heart didn't even pound.

Beside my kitchen table stood Christine, her eyes darting between me and the package of cocaine lying there, which I knew she recognized.

She might also have known the gun by sight. She had already heard me approaching, so I didn't startle her. Her eyes looked wide. Neither of us spoke for what seemed a long time.

Finally she asked, "Did you kill Wayne?" She said it faintly, yet trying to sound almost casual, trying to imply I could answer without expecting any reaction.

I started to answer, twice. She watched me, probably thinking of the day I'd come here and how little she had learned about me since then. Maybe she recalled details the detective told her about Wayne's death.

Either I lunged at her or I flailed and she took it the wrong way, but Christine snatched the gun off the table and fired it at me.

The first shot drilled through my right shoulder. I started to shout something. The second shot smashed my face. Everything went black, as if I'd been watching a TV and the tube had exploded.

A commercial I'd watched as a child came back to me. It was for a kid's cereal that had a bunch of cartoon monsters on the box. They weren't scary monsters but ugly, lumpy things that all lived in a giant tree, like a family. The music for the commercial had those bleating horns that TV movies use when they pretend it's the 1920s. Each one of the little monsters got to sing a line of the song. I'm sure I never ate this cereal, and I can't remember the name of it.

It went away. I became aware of someone wailing in pain, and then I could see my kitchen ceiling. Stupid was licking my face. I sat up. That wail in my ears was a siren somewhere close by.

Christine hadn't shot me in the face, exactly. She'd hit the side of my head. Part of my ear was gone. I couldn't hear on that side, and couldn't keep my balance. To pull myself up I needed the table.

"Come on," I said to the dogs.

After a struggle with the knob I opened the door to the side alley and let them out. They waited for me. My head really throbbed now. I pressed my left hand hard against it. Even though it hurt so bad, it seemed numb. I couldn't feel my fingers against my skin.

I fell against the house several times as we walked to the street. Crossing over the landing outside Pat's door I nearly tripped over a potted plant I'd never noticed there.

At last we reached the sidewalk.

"Go!" I told the dogs, and waved them away with my good hand. "Go away!"

They blinked at me.

I stamped the concrete. That gave them a start.

"Get out of here!" I said. There was more than one siren now, probably on Gentilly. "Go! They'll gas you at the pound! Go away!"

Useless understood more quickly, probably because he'd never really believed I'd keep them anyway. He started wandering away, that same tired pace street dogs have. But Stupid couldn't believe it. He cried.

A lot of blood started spraying out of my head. I collapsed onto the ground. The dogs took off before the cops found me.

CRESCENT CITY BOOKS
New Orleans, LA
www.blackwidowpress.com

*The Sound of Building Coffins* by Louis Maistros

*Stay Out of New Orleans: Strange Stories* by P. Curran

*The Breathtaking Christa P: A Novel of Crime* by P. Curran


THE VALENTIN ST. CYR MYSTERIES by David Fulmer


*Chasing the Devil's Tail*

*Jass*

*Rampart Street*

*Lost River*

*The Iron Angel*

*Eclipse Alley*

*The Day Ends at Dawn*